"Are you sure you ~~_____~~ **night, by yourself? If you're nervous, I could stay," Nate offered. "I'd sleep on the couch, I promise."**

"I'll be fine," Jamie insisted. "Go home."

"All right." He stepped onto the porch, but the sight of a dark-colored SUV cruising slowly by made him freeze. "Who's that?"

Jamie peered around him. "I don't know."

He switched off the porch light, plunging them into shadow as the vehicle drove slowly past. Though the driver was hard to make out, Nate was sure he turned his head to look at them.

"The license plate on the car is obscured," Jamie whispered.

Nate pulled her back into the house.

"Do you think that was him?" Jamie asked. "The man at the dance?"

"I don't know. It could have been." Nate pulled her close, his heart pounding. She didn't fight him, but relaxed in his embrace. "I'm not leaving you here alone."

"No." Her eyes searched his. Then she pressed her lips to his, her eyes still open, still locked to his.

COLD CONSPIRACY

CINDI MYERS

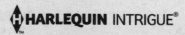

HARLEQUIN INTRIGUE®

To the ladies of GJWW.

ISBN-13: 978-1-335-60466-8

Cold Conspiracy

Copyright © 2019 by Cynthia Myers

Recycling programs
for this product may
not exist in your area.

Printed in U.S.A.

www.Harlequin.com

Cindi Myers is the author of more than fifty novels. When she's not crafting new romance plots, she enjoys skiing, gardening, cooking, crafting and daydreaming. A lover of small-town life, she lives with her husband and two spoiled dogs in the Colorado mountains.

Books by Cindi Myers

Harlequin Intrigue

Eagle Mountain Murder Mystery: Winter Storm Wedding

Eagle Mountain Murder Mystery

The Ranger Brigade: Family Secrets

The Men of Search Team Seven

Visit the Author Profile page at Harlequin.com.

CAST OF CHARACTERS

Jamie Douglas—Eagle Mountain's first female deputy is used to looking after herself and her sister.

Nate Hall—Nate split up with Jamie when he left town seven years ago. Now that he's returned, he's wondering how to bridge the gap between them.

Donna Douglas—Jamie's nineteen-year-old sister has Down syndrome, but longs for more independence.

Sheriff Travis Walker—With his wedding day nearing, Travis feels more pressure than ever to stop a killer.

The Ice Cold Killer—The serial killer is targeting women in and around Eagle Mountain.

Alex Woodruff—The college student and avid ice climber was a prime suspect for the murders until he left town.

Tim Dawson—Alex's best friend may be back in town, but why?

Pi Calendri—The high school student knows more about Alex and Tim than he's letting on.

Chapter One

"Come on, Donna. We need to head back to the house or I'll be late for work." Rayford County Sheriff's Deputy Jamie Douglas turned to look back at her nineteen-year-old sister, Donna, who was plodding up the forest trail in snowshoes. Short and plump, her brown curls like a halo peeking out from beneath her pink knit cap, cheeks rosy from the cold, Donna reminded Jamie of the Hummel figurines their grandmother had collected. On a Monday morning in mid-January, the two sisters had the forest to themselves, and Jamie had been happy to take advantage of a break in the weather to get outside and enjoy some exercise. But now that she needed to get home, Donna was in no rush, stopping to study a clump of snow on a tree branch alongside the trail, or laughing at the antics of Cheyenne, one of their three dogs. The twenty-pound terrier-Pomeranian mix was the smallest and easiest to handle of the canines, so Donna had charge of him. Jamie had a firm hold on the leashes for the other two—a Siberian husky named Targa, and a blond Lab mix, Cookie. "Donna!" Jamie called again, insistent.

Donna looked up, her knit cap slipping over one eye. "I'm coming!" she called, breaking into a clumsy jog.

"Don't run. You'll fall and hurt yourself." Jamie started back toward her sister, but had taken only a few steps when Donna tripped and went sprawling.

"Oh!" It was Jamie's turn to run—not an easy feat in snowshoes, though she managed to reach Donna's side quickly. "Are you okay?"

Donna looked up, tears streaming down her plump cheeks. "I'm all wet," she sniffed.

"Come on, let's get you up." Jamie took her sister's arm. "It's not far to the car." Though Down syndrome had delayed her development, Donna was only a few inches shorter than Jamie and outweighed her by twenty pounds. Getting her to her feet while both women were wearing snowshoes made for a clumsy undertaking. Add in three romping dogs, and by the time Donna was upright, both sisters were tired and damp.

Once she was assured Donna would stay on her feet, Jamie took charge of Cheyenne, adjusting her grip on all three leashes. But just then, something crashed through the undergrowth to their left. Barking and lunging, Targa tore from her grasp, quickly followed by Cookie and Cheyenne. All three dogs took off across the snow, on the trail of the mule deer buck who was bounding through the forest.

"A deer!" Donna clapped her hands. "Did you see him run?"

"Targa! Cookie! Come here!" Jamie called after the dogs, even as the clamor of their barking receded into the woods. Silently cursing her bad luck, she slipped off her pack and dropped it at Donna's feet. "Stay here," she ordered. "I'm going after the dogs."

Running in snowshoes was probably like dancing in clown shoes, Jamie thought as she navigated through the thick undergrowth. She could still hear the dogs—that was good. "Targa, come!" she shouted. She needed to find the dogs soon. Otherwise, she'd be showing up late for the mandatory meeting Sheriff Travis Walker had called, and she hated to think what he would have to say. As the department's newest deputy, she couldn't count on him cutting her much slack.

The dogs' tracks were easy to follow through the snow, which was churned up by their running paws. Here and there she spotted the imprints of the deer, too. She replayed the sight of the big animal crashing out of the woods toward them. What had made the buck run that way—before the dogs had even seen it? Was a mountain lion stalking the animal?

Fighting back a shiver of fear, she scanned the forest surrounding her. She saw nothing, but she couldn't shake a feeling of uneasiness—as if she really was being watched.

She crashed through the underbrush and emerged in a small clearing. The dogs were on the other side, all wagging tails and happy grins as they gathered around a man on snowshoes, who scowled at the three of them. Jamie's heart sank when she recognized the uniform of a wildlife officer—what some people called a game warden. He looked up at her approach. "Are these your dogs?" he asked.

"Yes, Nate. They're my dogs." She crossed the clearing to him and gathered up the leashes. Worse even than having her dogs caught in the act of breaking the law by a wildlife officer was being caught by Nate Hall. The big blond outdoorsman managed to look like a conquering Viking, even in his khaki uniform, though Jamie could remember when he had been a gawky boy. The two of them had been pretty successfully avoiding each other since he had moved back to Eagle Mountain four months ago, after an absence of seven years. "My sister fell and I was helping her up when they got away from me," Jamie said.

"Jamie, you ought to know better," Nate said. "The deer and elk are already stressed this winter, with the deep snow. Allowing dogs to chase them stresses them further and could even result in their death."

What made him think he had the right to lecture her? "I didn't *allow* the dogs to chase the deer," she said. "It was an accident." She glared down at the three dogs, who now sat at her feet, tongues lolling, the pictures of innocence.

"Hello!" They both turned to see Donna tromping toward them. She towed Jamie's pack behind her, dragging it through the snow by its strap.

"Donna, you were supposed to wait for me," Jamie said.

"I wanted to see what you were doing." Donna stopped, dropped the pack and turned to Nate. "Hello. I'm Donna. I'm Jamie's sister."

"Hello, Donna," Nate said. His gaze swept over Donna, assessing her. "Your sister said you fell. Are you okay?"

"Just wet." Donna looked down at the damp knees of her snow pants.

"We really need to be going." Jamie picked up her pack with one hand, while holding all three leashes in the other. "I have to get to work."

"Let me take the dogs." Not waiting for her reply, Nate stepped forward and took the leashes. She started to argue, then thought better of it. If the dogs got away from him, maybe he wouldn't be so quick to blame her.

"Nice day for snowshoeing," he said as he fell into step beside Jamie, Donna close behind.

She didn't really want to make small talk with him. The last real conversation they had had—seven years ago—had not been a pleasant one. Though she didn't remember much of anything either of them had said, she remembered the pain behind their words. The hurt had faded, leaving an unsettled feeling in its place.

The dogs trotted along like obedience school protégés. When Targa tried to pull on the leash, Nate reined her in with a firm "No!" and she meekly obeyed—something she never did for Jamie. Apparently, muscles and a deep, velvety voice worked to impress female canines, too.

"It's a beautiful day," Donna said. "It's supposed to be Jamie's day off, but now she has to go to work."

"Something come up?" he asked. His gray eyes met hers, clearly telegraphing the question he didn't want to voice in front of Donna—*Any more murders?* Over the past three weeks, a serial killer had taken the lives of five local women. Dubbed the Ice Cold Killer, because of the calling cards he left behind with the words *Ice Cold* printed on them, the serial murderer had eluded all attempts by local law enforcement to track him down. Heavy snow and avalanches that closed the only road out of town for weeks at a time had further hampered the investigation.

"Nothing new," Jamie said. "The sheriff has called a meeting to go over everything we know so far."

Nate nodded and faced forward again. "When I moved back to town I was surprised to find out you were a sheriff's deputy," he said. "I never knew you were interested in law enforcement."

"There's a lot you never knew about me." She hadn't meant the words to come out so sharply and hurried to smooth them over. Otherwise, Nate might think she was still carrying a torch for him. "I stopped by the department one day to get an application to become a 911 dispatcher," she said. "I found out they were recruiting officers. They especially wanted women and would pay for my training, as long as I agreed to stay with the department three years. The starting salary was a lot more than I could make as a dispatcher, and I thought the work sounded interesting." She shrugged. "And it is."

"A little too interesting, sometimes, I imagine," Nate said.

"Well, yeah. Lately, at least." She had been one of the first on the scene when the killer's third victim, Fiona Winslow, had been found. Before then, she had never seen the body of someone who had died violently. Then she had responded to the call about a body in a car in the high school parking lot and found the killer's most recent victim, teacher Anita Allbritton. The deaths had shocked her, but they had also made her more determined than ever to do what she could to stop this killer.

"The sheriff is getting married soon," Donna said.

"Yes, he is." Nate looked back at her. "I'm going to be in the wedding."

"You are?" Donna sounded awed, as if Nate had announced that he was going to fly to the moon.

"I'm one of the groomsmen," Nate said.

"I didn't know you knew Travis that well," Jamie said.

"We ended up rooming together in college for a while," Nate said. "He's really the one who talked me into coming back to Eagle Mountain, when an opening came up in my department."

So Nate had returned to his hometown because of Travis—not because of anyone else he had left behind.

They reached the trailhead, where Jamie's SUV was parked. Nate helped her get the dogs into the vehicle. "Where is your car?" Donna asked, looking around the empty parking area.

"I hiked over from the base of Mount Wilson," Nate said. "I'm checking on the condition of the local deer and elk herds. The department is thinking of setting up some feeding stations, to help with survival rates this winter. All this snow is making it tough for even the elk to dig down and get enough food."

"I could help feed deer!" Donna's face lit up.

"I appreciate the offer," Nate said. "But they're too wild to come to people. We put out pelleted food and hay in areas where the animals congregate, and monitor them with remote cameras."

Nate had intended to study wildlife biology in college, Jamie remembered. He was in his element out here in the snowy woods. That his job involved carrying a gun and arresting poachers would only make the work more interesting to him. He had always had a strong sense of wrong and right. Some people might even call him idealistic.

She didn't have much room for idealism in her life these days—she had to focus on being practical. "We have to go," she said, tossing her pack in after the dogs and shutting the hatch. "Buckle up, Donna."

She started around the side of the car to the driver's seat, but Nate blocked her way. "I'm glad I ran into you this afternoon," he said. "We didn't have much chance to visit at the scavenger hunt at the Walker Ranch."

She shook her head. Fiona Winslow had died that day—no one had been in a visiting mood. "I'm sure we'll run into each other from time to time," she said. Eagle Mountain was a small town in a remote area—

she saw a lot of the same people over and over again, whether she wanted to or not. "But don't get any ideas about picking up where we left off." She shoved past him and opened the car door.

After she made sure Donna was buckled in, she backed the SUV out of the lot. Donna waved to Nate, who returned the wave, though the look on his face wasn't an especially friendly one.

Donna sat back in her seat. "He was cuuuute!" she said.

"Don't you remember Nate?" Jamie asked. "He used to come over to the house sometimes, when he and I were in middle school and high school."

"I remember boys," Donna said. "He's a man. You should go out with him."

"I'm not going out with anybody," Jamie said. She wasn't going to deny that Nate was good-looking. He had been handsome in high school, but time and working out, or maybe the demands of his job, had filled out and hardened his physique. Though the bulky parka and pack he had on today didn't reveal much, the jeans and sweater he had worn to the party at the ranch had showed off his broad shoulders and narrow waist in a way that had garnered second and third looks from most of the women present.

"Why don't you have a boyfriend?" Donna asked. It wasn't a new question. Donna seemed determined to pair up her sister with any number of men in town.

"I'm too busy to have a boyfriend," Jamie said. "I work and I take care of you, and I don't need anyone else."

"But I want you to have a boyfriend," Donna said.

"Sorry to disappoint you."

"I have a boyfriend!" Donna grinned and hugged herself.

"Oh?" This was the first Jamie had heard that Donna was interested in anyone in particular. "Who is your boyfriend?"

"Henry. He works in produce."

Donna worked part-time bagging groceries at Eagle Mountain Grocery. Jamie made a note to stop by the store and check out Henry. Was he another special-needs young adult like Donna, or the local teen heartthrob—or even an adult who might have unknowingly attracted her? It was an easy mistake for people to think of Donna as a perpetual child, but she was a young woman, and it was up to Jamie to see to it that no one took advantage of her.

She slowed to pass a blue Chevy parked half off the road. The car hadn't been there when they had come this way earlier. If she had more time, she would stop and check it out, but a glance at the clock on the dash showed she was cutting it close if she was going to drop Donna off at Mrs. Simmons's house and change into her sheriff's department uniform before the meeting.

"What is wrong with that car?" Donna looked back over her shoulder. "We should stop and see."

"I'll let the sheriff's office know about it," Jamie said. "They'll send someone out to check."

"I really think we should stop." Donna's expressive face was twisted with genuine concern. "Someone might be hurt."

"I didn't see anyone with the car," Jamie said.

"You didn't stop and look!" Donna leaned toward her, pleading. "We need to go back. Please? What if the car broke and someone is there, all cold and freezing?"

Her sister's compassion touched Jamie. The world would be a better place if there were more people like Donna in it. She slowed and pulled to the shoulder, preparing to make a U-turn. "All right. We'll go back." Maybe the sheriff would accept stopping to check on a disabled vehicle as an excuse for her tardiness.

She drove past the car, then turned back and pulled in behind it, angling her vehicle slightly, just as if she had been in a department cruiser instead of her personal vehicle. "Stay in the car," she said to Donna, who was reaching for the buckle on her seat belt.

Donna's hand stilled. "Okay," she said.

Cautiously, Jamie approached the vehicle. Though she didn't usually walk around armed, since the appearance of the Ice Cold Killer, she wore a gun in a holster on her belt at all times. Its presence eased some of her nervousness now. The late-model blue Chevrolet Malibu sat parked crookedly, nose toward the snowbank on the side of the road, the snow around it churned by footsteps, as if a bunch of people had hastily parked it and piled out.

She leaned forward, craning to see into the back seat, but nothing appeared out of order there. But something wasn't right. The hair rose up on the back of her neck and she put a hand on the gun, ready to draw it if necessary.

But she didn't need a gun to defend herself from the person in the car. The woman lay on her back across the front seat, eyes staring at nothing, the blood already dried from the wound on her throat.

Chapter Two

Nate reached his truck parked at the base of Mount Wilson just as his radio crackled. Though a recently installed repeater facilitated radio transmission in this remote area, the pop and crackle of heavy static often made the messages difficult to understand. He could make out something about needing an officer to assist the sheriff's department. He keyed the mic and replied. "This is Officer Hall. What was that location again?"

"Forest Service Road 1410. That's one-four-one-zero."

"Copy that. I'm on my way." The trailhead on 1410 was where he had left Jamie and her sister. Had they found something? Or had something happened to them?

He pressed down harder on the gas pedal, snow flying up around the truck as he raced down the narrow path left by the snowplow. The Ice Cold Killer's next to last victim, Lauren Grenado, had been found on a Forest Service road not that far from here. Maybe Nate shouldn't have left Jamie and her sister alone.

He could have asked them to give him a ride back to his truck, as an excuse to stay with them. But Jamie had said she was running late for work, so she probably would have turned him down.

Who was he kidding? She definitely would have turned him down. She clearly didn't want anything to do with him, apparently still holding a grudge over their breakup all those years ago.

And yeah, maybe he hadn't handled that so well—but he'd been nineteen and headed off to college out of state. He had thought he was doing the right thing by ending their relationship when it was impossible for them to be together. He had told himself that eventually she would see the sense in splitting up. Maybe she would even thank him one day. But she wasn't thanking him for anything—the knowledge that he could have hurt her that deeply chafed at him like a stone in his boot.

He spotted her SUV up ahead, parked behind a blue sedan. Jamie, hands in the pockets of her parka, paced alongside the road. He didn't see Donna—she was probably in the car.

He pulled in behind Jamie's SUV and turned on his flashers. Jamie whirled to face him. "What are you doing here?" she demanded.

"I got a call to assist the sheriff's department." He joined her and nodded toward the car. "What have you got?"

"Another dead woman." Her voice was flat, as was her expression. But he caught the note of despair at the end of the sentence and recognized the pain shin-

ing out from her hazel eyes. He had a sharp impulse
to pull her close and comfort her—but he knew right
away that would be a very bad idea. She wasn't his
friend and former lover Jamie right now. She was
Deputy Douglas, a fellow officer who needed him
to do his job.

"I've got emergency flashers in my car," he said.
He glanced toward her SUV. Donna sat in the front
seat, hunched over and rocking back and forth. "Is
your sister okay?"

"She's upset. Crying. Better to leave her alone for
a bit."

"Do you know who the woman is?"

She shook her head. "No. But I think it's the Ice
Cold Killer. I didn't open the door or anything, but
she looks like his other victims—throat cut, wrists
and ankles wrapped with tape."

He walked back to his truck, retrieved the emergency beacons and set them ten yards behind his
bumper and ten yards ahead of the car. As he passed,
he glanced into the front seat and caught a glimpse
of the dead woman, staring up at him. Suppressing a
shudder, he returned to Jamie, as a Rayford County
Sheriff's cruiser approached. The driver parked on
the opposite side of the road, and tall and lanky Deputy Dwight Prentice got out. "Travis is on his way,"
he said, when they had exchanged greetings.

"I was headed back to town to get ready for our
meeting when I saw the car," Jamie said. "It wasn't
here when I drove by earlier, on my way to the Pick-
axe snowshoe trail."

"The meeting has been pushed back to four o'clock." Dwight walked over to the car and peered inside. "Do you know who she is?"

"I don't recognize her, and I never opened the car door," Jamie said. "I figured I should wait for the crime scene team."

"Did you call in the license plate?" Dwight asked.

Jamie flushed. "No. I… I didn't think of it."

"I'll do it," Nate said.

Radio transmission was clearer here and after a few minutes he was back with Jamie and Dwight, with a name. "The car is registered to Michaela Underwood of Ames, Iowa."

The sound of an approaching vehicle distracted them. No one said anything as Sheriff Travis Walker pulled in behind Dwight's cruiser. Tall and trim, looking like a law enforcement recruiting poster, the young sheriff showed the strain of the hunt for this serial killer in the shadows beneath his eyes and the grim set of his mouth. He pulled on gloves as he crossed to them, and listened to Jamie's story. "What time did you drive by here on your way to the trail?" he asked.

"I left my house at five after nine, so it would have been about nine thirty," she said.

"Your call came in at eleven fifty-two," Travis said. "How long was that after you found her?"

"I had to drive until I found a signal, but it wasn't that long," Jamie said. "We stopped here at eleven forty-five. I know because I kept checking the time, worried I was going to be late for work."

Travis glanced toward her car. "Who is that with you?"

"My sister, Donna. She never got out of the car." One of the dogs—the big husky—stuck its head out of the partially opened driver's-side window. "I have my dogs with me, too," Jamie added.

"All right. Let's see what we've got."

The others stood back as Travis opened the driver's-side door. He leaned into the vehicle and emerged a few moments later with a small card, like a business card, and held it up for them to see. The bold black letters were easy to read at this short distance: ICE COLD. "Butch is on his way," Travis said. Butch Collins, a retired doctor, served as Rayford County's medical examiner. "Once he's done, Dwight and I will process the scene. I've got a wrecker on standby to take the car to our garage."

"It must be getting crowded in there," Nate said—which earned him a deeper frown from the sheriff.

"Nate, can you stay and handle traffic, in case we get any lookie-loos?" Travis asked.

"Sure."

"What do you want me to do?" Jamie asked.

"Take your sister home. I'll see you at the station this afternoon. You can file your statement then."

"All right."

Nate couldn't tell if she was relieved to be dismissed—or upset about being excluded. He followed her back to her SUV and walked around to the passenger side. The dogs began barking but quieted at a reprimand from Jamie. Donna eased the door open a crack at Nate's approach. "Hello," Nate said. He had a vague memory of Donna as a sweet, awkward little girl. She wasn't so little anymore.

"Hello." She glanced toward the blue sedan, where Dwight and Travis still stood. "Did you see the woman?"

"She's not anyone we know," Nate said. "A tourist, probably." More than a few visitors had been stranded in Eagle Mountain when Dixon Pass, the only route into town, closed due to repeated avalanches triggered by the heavy snowfall.

"Why did she have to die?" Donna asked.

Because there are bad people in the world, he thought. But that didn't seem the right answer to give this girl, who wanted reassurance. "I don't know," he said. "But your sister and I, and Sheriff Walker and all his deputies, are going to do everything we can to find the person who hurt her."

Donna's eyes met his—sweet, sad eyes. "I like you," she said.

"I like you, too," he answered, touched.

"All right, Donna. Quit flirting with Nate so he can get back to work." Jamie turned the key in the ignition and started the SUV.

"You okay, Jamie?" he asked.

The look she gave him could have lit a campfire. "Why wouldn't I be okay?" she asked. "I'm a deputy. I know how to handle myself."

"I wasn't implying you didn't." He took a step back. "But this kind of thing shakes up everybody. If you asked the sheriff, he'd probably tell you he's upset." At least, Nate had known Travis long enough to recognize the signs that this case was tearing him up inside.

"I'm fine," Jamie said, not looking at him. "And I need to go."

Look me in the eye and let me see that you're really okay, he thought. But he only took another step back and watched as she drove away. Then he walked into the road, to flag down the ambulance he could see in the distance.

JAMIE SHIFTED IN the driver's seat of the SUV, as uncomfortable as if her clothes were too tight. Nate had looked at her as if he expected her to dissolve into tears at any minute. He ought to know she wasn't like that. She was tough—and a lot tougher now than she was when they had been a couple. She had had to develop a thick skin to deal with everything life had thrown at her.

She was a sheriff's deputy, and she had seen dead people before. She wasn't going to fall apart at the sight of a body. Though she had forgotten to call in the license plate of the car, which she should have done, even if she wasn't on duty. And she should have stayed and helped process the crime scene.

If she had been a man, would the sheriff have asked her to stay? No, she decided, her gender didn't have anything to do with this. Travis Walker was as fair a man as she had ever known. But she had had Donna with her. She had to look after her sister, and the sheriff knew that. They had discussed her situation before he hired her. With their parents dead and no other relatives living nearby, Jamie was responsible for Donna, and might be for the rest of her life. While Donna might one day want to live on her own, with some assistance, most programs that would allow that were only available in larger cities—not small towns like Eagle Mountain. As long as Donna wanted to stay in their childhood home, Jamie would do whatever she could to make that happen.

She was happy to take care of her sister, but it meant making certain adjustments. She wasn't free to go out whenever she liked. She couldn't be spontaneous, because she had to make sure Donna was safe and looked after. She didn't think many men her age would be open to that kind of life.

Which was fine. She didn't need a man to make her complete.

She didn't need Nate Hall. When his plans changed and he decided to go away for college, he had shed her as easily as if he had been getting rid of last year's winter coat or a pair of shoes he'd outgrown.

He had told her he loved her, but when you loved someone, you didn't treat them like you were doing them a favor when you said goodbye.

"I'm hungry. We missed lunch."

Jamie guessed Donna wasn't too traumatized, if she was thinking about food. "I'll make you a sandwich before I drop you off at Mrs. Simmons's," she said. "I think there's still some tuna in the refrigerator. Would you like that?"

"I don't want to go to Mrs. Simmons's house," Donna said. "I want to stay home."

"I have to work this afternoon," Jamie said. "And I may be late. You can't stay in the house by yourself."

"Why not?" Donna asked. "I know how to dial 911 if something bad happens."

Jamie tightened her hands on the steering wheel until her knuckles ached. "It's not safe for you to stay by yourself," she said. Even if Donna's mental capacity had matched her physical age, Jamie wouldn't have wanted to leave her alone. Not with a killer preying on women in Eagle Mountain.

"I'm old enough to stay home by myself," Donna said.

"Mrs. Simmons's feelings will be hurt if you don't stay with her," Jamie said. For sure, their older neighbor would miss the money Jamie paid her to watch over Donna while Jamie worked.

"You could explain it to her." But Donna sounded doubtful. She was very sensitive to other people's feelings—perhaps because her own had been wounded so often by unthinking remarks.

"If you don't go see her, you'll miss your shows," Jamie said. Every afternoon, Mrs. Simmons and Donna watched old sitcoms and dramas on a classic TV station. Since Jamie didn't subscribe to the expensive cable package required for such programming, Mrs. Simmons was Donna's only source for her beloved shows.

Donna sighed—a long, dramatic sigh that would have done any teen girl proud. "I guess I had better go, then."

"Thank you." Jamie leaned over and squeezed her sister's arm. "I really appreciate you being so nice about it."

"What time will you be home?" Donna asked.

"I don't know. I have this meeting, but if the sheriff wants me to work after that, I will." She sat up straighter, her next words as much a pep talk for herself as for her sister. "The work I do is important. I'm helping to keep people safe." Though she and her fellow deputies hadn't been able to keep Michaela Underwood and the Ice Cold Killer's other victims safe. The knowledge hurt, and it goaded her to do more. To do better.

"Will you see Nate at the meeting?" Donna asked.

Jamie frowned. "Nate is a wildlife officer—he doesn't work for the sheriff's department."

"He's nice," Donna said. "And cute."

"You think every man you see is cute," Jamie teased.

"I don't think Mr. McAdams is cute." Donna made a face. Mr. McAdams was the meat market manager at Eagle Mountain Grocery. Jamie had to admit he bore a startling resemblance to the photo of last year's Grand Champion steer that graced the door to the meat freezer at the grocery.

"Is Henry cute?" Jamie asked.

Donna grinned. "Oh, yeah. Henry is cuuuute!" She dissolved into giggles, and Jamie couldn't help giggling, too. She could never feel gloomy for long when she was with Donna. Her sister had a real gift for bringing joy into the lives of everyone she knew.

They reached home and the dogs piled out of the SUV and raced into the house, then out into the backyard, through the dog door Jamie's father had installed years before. Three laps around the yard, noses to the ground, then they were back inside, lined up in formation in front of the treat cabinet. "Treat!" Donna proclaimed and took out the bag that held the beloved bacon snacks. She carefully doled out one to each dog, pronouncing "Good dog!" as each treat was devoured.

The next hour passed in a blur of lunch, changing clothes and hustling Donna two houses down to Mrs. Simmons, who met them at the door, a worried expression on her face. "There's some cookies for you on the table," Mrs. Simmons said to Donna. "You go get them while I talk to Jamie."

When Donna had left them, Mrs. Simmons said, keeping her voice low. "I heard they found another woman's body."

"Yes." There was no sense denying it. Half the town listened to the emergency scanner, the way some people listened to music on the radio. "I don't know anything to tell you," she added quickly, before Mrs. Simmons could press her for more information.

"I never thought I'd see the day when I didn't feel safe around here," Mrs. Simmons said.

Jamie wanted to reassure the woman that she would be fine—that there was nothing to worry about. But with six women dead and the department no closer to finding the killer, the words would be empty and meaningless. "I have to go," she said. "I'm not sure how late I'll be. If it will be later than nine, I'll call you."

"Don't worry about us," Mrs. Simmons said. "Donna is welcome to spend the night if she needs to. She's good company."

Ten minutes later, Jamie parked her SUV in the lot behind the sheriff's department. She stowed her purse in her locker and made her way down the hall to the conference room. Dwight and Travis's brother, Deputy Gage Walker, were already there, along with Ryder Stewart from Colorado State Patrol, and US Marshal Cody Rankin, his arm in a sling.

"How's the arm?" Jamie asked as she took a seat at the table across from Cody.

"The arm's fine. The shoulder hurts where they took the bullet out, but I'll live." He had been shot by an ex-con who had been pursuing him and the woman who was catering Travis's upcoming wedding. "I'm not officially on duty," Cody added. "But Travis asked me to sit in and contribute what I could."

The sheriff entered and everyone moved to seats around the table. Though newspaper reports almost always included at least one reference to the sheriff's "boyish good looks," today he looked much older, like a combat veteran who has seen too many battles. He walked to the bulletin board in the center of the wall facing the conference table and pinned up an eight-by-ten glossy photo of a smiling, dark-haired woman.

The image joined five others of similarly smiling, pretty females. The victims of the Ice Cold Killer.

"Her name is Michaela Underwood," Travis said. "Twenty-two years old, she moved to Eagle Mountain to live near her parents. She recently started a new job at the bank." He turned to face them. "These killings have got to stop," he said. "And they have to stop now."

Chapter Three

The meeting at the sheriff's department had already begun when Nate arrived. He slipped into the empty seat next to Jamie. She glanced at him, her expression unreadable, then turned her attention back to the sheriff, who was speaking.

"We're putting every resource we've got behind this case," Travis said. "We're going to look at every bit of evidence again. We're going to reinterview everyone even remotely connected with the women who died, everyone in the areas where they were killed—anyone who might have possibly seen or heard anything."

"What about suspects?" Nate asked. He indicated a board on the far left side of the room, where photos of several men were pinned.

"Where we can, we'll talk to them again." Travis said. "We've ruled them out as the murderers, but they may know something." He rested his pointer on photos of a pair of young men at the top of the chart. "Alex Woodruff and Tim Dawson drew our attention because they were at the Walking W Ranch the day the third victim, Fiona Winslow, was killed. They didn't have an alibi for the previous two murders, of Kelly Farrow and Christy O'Brien. Once the road re-opened, they disappeared. I'm still trying to confirm that they returned to Fort Collins, where they're supposedly attending Colorado State University."

He shifted the pointer to a photo of a handsome, dark-haired man. "Ken Rutledge came to our attention because he lived next door to Kelly Farrow and had dated her business partner, Darcy Marsh. When he attacked Darcy several times and eventually kidnapped her, we thought we had found our killer. But since his arrest, there have been three more murders."

Quickly, Travis summarized the case against the remaining suspects—three high school students who had been seen the night Christy O'Brien was murdered, and a veterinarian who resented Kelly Farrow and Darcy Marsh setting up a competing veterinary practice. "They all have solid alibis for most of the murders, so we had to rule them out," he concluded.

He moved back to the head of the conference table. "We're putting together profiles of all the victims, to see if we can find any common ground, and we're constructing a detailed timeline. If you're not out on a call, then I want you studying the evidence, looking for clues and trying to anticipate this killer's next move."

They all murmured agreement.

"Some of this we've already done," Travis said. "But we're going to do it again. The person who did this left clues that tell us who he is. It's up to us to find them. Colorado Bureau of Investigation has agreed to send an investigator to work with us when the road opens again, but we don't know when that will be. Until then, we're on our own. I want to start by considering some questions."

He picked up a marker and wrote on a whiteboard to the left of the women's pictures, speaking as he wrote. "Why is this killer—or killers—here?"

"Because he lives here," Gage said.

"Because he was visiting here and got caught by the snow," Dwight added.

"Because he came here to kill someone specific and found out he liked it," Jamie said. She flushed as the others turned to look at her. "It would be one way to confuse authorities about one specific murder," she said. "By committing a bunch of unrelated ones."

Travis nodded and added this to their list of reasons.

"Are we talking about one man working alone, or two men working together?" Ryder asked.

"That was my next question." Travis wrote it on the whiteboard.

"I think it has to be two," Gage said. "The timing of some of the killings—Christy O'Brien, Fiona Winslow and Anita Allbritton, in particular—required everything to be carried out very quickly. The woman had to be subdued, bound, killed and put into her vehicle. One man would have a hard time doing that."

"Maybe he's a really big guy," Cody said. "Really powerful—powerful enough to overwhelm and subdue the women."

"I agree with Gage that I think we're probably looking at two men," Travis said. "But that should make it easier to catch them. And if we find one, that will probably lead us to the second one." He turned to write on the board again. "What do we know for certain about these murders?"

"The victims are all women," Dwight said. "Young women—all of them under forty, most under thirty."

"They're all killed out of doors," Nate said. "Away from other people."

"Except for Fiona," Jamie said. "There were a lot of people around when she was killed."

"They were all left in vehicles, except Fiona," Ryder said. "And they were alone in their vehicles."

"The killer uses the weather to his advantage," Gage said. "The snow makes travel difficult and covers up his tracks."

"I think he likes to taunt law enforcement," Ryder said. "He leaves those cards, knowing we'll find them."

"He wants us to know he's committing the murders, but is that really taunting?" Dwight asked.

"He killed Fiona at the Walker Ranch," Gage said. "When the place was crawling with cops." He shifted to look at Jamie and Nate. "I wouldn't be surprised if he knew the two of you were nearby when he killed Michaela this morning."

Jamie gasped. "That deer!"

Nate touched her arm. "What deer?"

"When my sister and I were on the trail this morning, a buck burst out of the underbrush suddenly, as if something had startled it," she said. "That's what my dogs were chasing. I wondered at the time if a mountain lion was after it. And when I was trying to catch the dogs I felt…unsettled." Her eyes met his, tinged with fear. "As if someone was watching me."

"That could be a good thing, if he thinks he's taunting us," Travis said. "We might be able to draw him out into the open."

"So far he's been very good at evading us," Gage said.

"He has, but from now on, we're going to be better." Travis pointed to Nate. "Did you see anyone else when you were in the area near the murder this morning?"

"I talked to an ice fisherman—checked his fishing license. A local guy." He searched his memory. "Abel Crutchfield."

"Gage, find him and interview him," Travis said.

Gage nodded.

"Anyone else?" Travis asked.

Nate shook his head. "Nobody else—except Jamie—Deputy Douglas—and her sister."

"Jamie, did you see anyone while you and your sister were out there?"

"No one," she admitted. "We didn't even pass any cars once we turned off the main highway."

"You start with the women," Travis told her. "See if you can find any commonalities—or any one woman who had a reason someone might want to kill her. Enough that he would kill others to cover up the crime."

"Yes, sir."

Travis gave the others their assignments—Nate was going to work with Gage on re-canvassing people who might have been in the vicinity of the two murders that occurred on forest service land.

The meeting ended and they filed out of the conference room, unsmiling and mostly silent. Nate stayed close to Jamie. "Is Donna upset about all this?" he asked.

"A little." She shook her head. "Not too much. She does a good job of living in the moment, and I try to keep things low-key—not bring the job home or act upset around her."

"These killings have everyone on edge," he said.

"It's frustrating, having him do this right under our noses. I realize it might be more than one person, but it's awkward to keep saying 'killer or killers.'"

"I get that," Nate said. "We all say 'he,' even though we suspect more than one person is involved."

"This is a small community," Jamie said. "We ought to be able to spot someone like this."

"He knows how to blend in," Nate said. "Or to hide."

She rolled her shoulders, as if shrugging off some burden. "I was surprised to see you here this afternoon," she said.

"The sheriff asked me to sit in. I've been one of the first on the scene for three of the murders. I spend a lot of time in the backcountry, where several of the women were found. He's trying to pull in every resource that might help. And I want to help. There's not a law enforcement officer in the county who doesn't want to catch this guy."

"Of course. Well, I'd better get to work. I'm going to start reviewing all the information we have about the victims." She started to turn away, but Nate touched her arm, stopping her.

"Now that I'm back in Eagle Mountain, I'd really like us to be friends again," he said.

The look she leveled at him held a decided chill. "I don't have a lot of time for hanging out and reminiscing about the old days," she said.

She shrugged out of his grasp and started down the hall but was stopped by Adelaide Kinkaid. The seventy-something office manager alternately nagged and nurtured the sheriff and his deputies, and kept her finger on the pulse of the town. She peered over the tops of her purple bifocals at Jamie. "Where's the sheriff?" she asked. "There's someone here to see him."

"I think he's still in the conference room, talking to Gage," Jamie said.

"I'll get him." Adelaide started to move past Jamie, then said, "You go on up front and stay with the couple who are waiting. I'm thinking this might benefit from a woman's touch."

Nate followed Jamie into the small front lobby of the sheriff's department. A man and a woman in their early thirties huddled together near the door, arms around each other, the man's head bent close to the woman's. They both looked up when Jamie and Nate arrived, the woman's face a mask of sorrow, her eyes puffy and red from crying.

"I'm Deputy Douglas." Jamie introduced herself. "The sheriff will be here shortly. Can I help you in the meantime?"

"We're Drew and Sarah Michener." The man offered his hand. "We came to find out everything we could about…about Michaela Underwood's death." He looked down at his wife, who had bowed her head and was dabbing at her eyes with a crumpled tissue. "We just heard the news, from her parents."

"Michaela is…was…my sister," the woman Sarah—said. "We heard she was killed in the woods near here this morning. I want to know if that man— Al—killed her."

"Who is Al?" Jamie asked.

"The man she was supposed to meet this morning, to go snowshoeing," Sarah said. "If you found her by herself, and he wasn't there, he must have been the one to kill her."

"I'm Sheriff Walker." Travis joined them in the lobby. "I understand you wanted to talk to me."

"This is Drew and Sarah Michener." Jamie made the introductions. "Michaela Underwood's sister and brother-in-law."

Travis shook hands with the Micheners. "We'd better talk about this in my office," he said. Jamie started to turn away, but Travis stopped her. "Deputy Douglas, you come, too."

Nate moved aside to let them pass, Travis leading the way to his office, Jamie bringing up the rear.

Gage joined him in the lobby. "What's up?" he asked, watching the couple disappear into Travis's office.

"Michaela's sister and her husband think they know who killed her," Nate said. "Or at least, she was supposed to meet a man—someone named Al— to go snowshoeing this morning."

"And you didn't see any sign of him out there with her, did you?" Gage asked.

"No." He continued to study the closed door, wishing he could hear what was going on in there. "Even if he didn't kill Michaela, the sheriff is going to want to find him and talk to him."

Gage put his hand on Nate's shoulder. "Right now, the sheriff wants me to talk to this ice fisherman, Abel Crutchfield. You up for coming with me?"

"Sure." He'd planned to finish his report on the condition of elk and deer herds in the area, but that could wait. A murder investigation took precedence over everything.

JAMIE FOLLOWED THE Micheners into Travis's office, closing the door after her. She stood by the door, while the Micheners occupied the two chairs in front of Travis's desk. Even if Jamie could have found more seating, there wasn't room for it in the small room.

Travis settled behind the desk, a neat, uncluttered space with only a laptop and a stack of files visible. "I'm very sorry for your loss," he said. "Losing a loved one is always hard, but losing them to murder is especially tough. We're doing everything we can to find who did this, but if you have anything you think can help us, we certainly want to know."

Sarah looked at her husband, who cleared his throat. "Can you tell us more about what you already know?" he asked. "We got the call this morning from Sarah's father— Michaela lived with them, so I assume that's how you knew to contact them. But they're understandably upset and didn't have a lot of details."

"We found Michaela's body in her vehicle on the side of Forest Service Road 1410," Travis said. "The medical examiner thinks she was killed earlier this morning. Do you know why she would have been in that area?"

"She had a date to go snowshoeing with a man," Sarah said. "Someone named Al. I don't know his last name." She leaned forward, clenched hands pressed to her chest. "I told her not to go out with someone she didn't know—especially not to someplace where there weren't a lot of other people around. Especially not with this…this madman going around killing women. But she wouldn't listen to me." Her face crumpled. "If only she had listened."

Drew rubbed his wife's back as she struggled to pull herself together. "Michaela was young," he said. "Only twenty-two. And she trusted people. She still thought she was invincible."

"How did she meet this man?" Travis asked.

Sarah sniffed, straightening her shoulders. "She met him at the bank. She just started the job on the first of the month. She's a teller. I guess they flirted, and the next day he came back and asked her out. She said…she said he was really nice and cute, and that she thought the idea of going snowshoeing was fun, and would be a good way to get to know each other without a lot of pressure."

"When was this—when they met?" Travis asked.

"I think it was Thursday when he first came into the bank." Sarah nodded. "Yes, Thursday. Because Friday she and I met for lunch and she told me about him—then she called me later that day to tell me he'd come back in and they'd made a date for Monday. She had the day off, and I guess he did, too."

"Did she say where he worked?" Travis asked. "Or what kind of work he did?"

"No." Sarah sighed. "I asked her that, too. She said she didn't know and it didn't matter, because that was the kind of thing they could get to know about each other on Monday. She told me I was too uptight and I worried too much. But I was right to worry! He must have been the one who killed her."

"What time were they supposed to meet?" Travis asked. "Or did he arrange to pick her up at your parents' house?"

"She said they were meeting at eight thirty at the trailhead for the snowshoe trails," Sarah said. "She told me she was being smart, driving herself, because if the date didn't go well, it would be easy for her to leave."

Travis looked to Jamie. "You said you got to the trailhead about nine thirty?"

"Yes," Jamie said. "There wasn't anyone else there.

And no other cars in the parking area. We didn't pass any cars on the way in, either."

"Her parents said she left their house at eight," Drew volunteered.

"She didn't tell them she was meeting a man," Sarah said. "Just that she was going snowshoeing with friends."

Travis nodded. "Tell me everything your sister said to you about this man—even if you don't think it's important. Did she describe what he looked like? Did she say where he lived, or if he gave her his phone number?"

"She just said he was cute. And funny. I guess he made some joke about how nobody could rob the bank with the road closed, because they wouldn't be able to go very far and she thought that was funny."

"What was he doing at the bank that day?" Travis asked. "Was he making a deposit or cashing a check?"

"I don't know. Sorry. I don't know if she had his number, though I think she said she gave him hers." She shook her head. "I've been thinking and thinking about this ever since we got the call from my dad, and there really isn't anything else. She got kind of defensive when I started quizzing her about the guy, and I didn't want to make her mad, so I changed the subject. I made her promise to call me when she got back to the house and let me know how things went, but I wasn't worried when I didn't hear from her by lunch. I just figured they were having a good time and decided to go eat together. But all that time, she was already dead." She covered her hand with her mouth and took a long, hiccupping breath.

Travis took a box of tissues from a drawer of his desk and slid it over to her. "Thank you for coming to talk to us," he said. "We'll follow up with the bank, see if anyone there remembers this man. If we're lucky, he'll be on the security footage. And we may want to talk to you and to your parents again."

"Of course," Drew said. He stood and helped his wife to her feet, also. "Please keep us posted on how things are going."

"We will." Travis came around the desk to escort the Micheners to the lobby. Jamie stepped aside, then followed them into the hall. She was still standing there, reviewing everything the Micheners had said, when Travis returned.

"I've got Dwight checking Michaela's phone records for a call or text that might be from Al," he said. "Meanwhile, I want you to come to the bank with me. I'll call Tom Babcock and ask him to meet us there. We need to get those security tapes and see what this guy looks like. Maybe we'll recognize him."

"Do you really think he's the Ice Cold Killer?" Jamie quickened her steps to keep up with the sheriff's long strides.

"He's the best lead we've had so far," Travis said. "I'm not going to let him get away."

Chapter Four

Abel Crutchfield lived in a mobile home on the west side of town that backed up to the river. His truck sat beneath a steel carport next to the trailer home, which was painted a cheerful turquoise and white. A trio of garden gnomes poked out of the snow around the bottom of the front steps, and a Christmas wreath with a drooping red ribbon still adorned the door.

Abel answered Gage's knock and his eyes widened at the sight of the two officers on his doorstep. "Is something wrong?" he asked.

"We'd like to ask you a few questions." Gage handed him a business card.

Abel read it, then looked past Gage to Nate. "You're the game warden I talked to this morning, aren't you?"

"Yes." Nate gave him a reassuring smile. "This isn't about that. We're hoping you can help us with something else."

"You'd better come in." Abel pushed open the screened door. "No sense standing out in the cold."

The front room of the trailer was neat but packed

with furniture—a sofa and two recliners, a large entertainment unit with a television and a stereo system, and two tall bookshelves filled with paperback books and ceramic figurines of dogs, bears, more gnomes, angels and others Nate couldn't make out. Abel threaded his way through the clutter and sat in one of the recliners and motioned to the sofa. "It's my wife's afternoon for her knitting club," he said. "So I'm here by myself. What can I help you with?"

"Did you see anyone else while you were fishing this morning?" Gage asked.

"Nope. I had the lake to myself."

"What about on the way to and from the lake?" Nate asked. "Did you see anyone on the road, or in the parking area?"

"What's this about?" Abel asked. "Not that it makes any difference in my answers, but I'd like to know."

"Another young woman was killed in that area this morning," Gage said.

Abel sat back, clearly shocked. "You don't think I killed her, do you?" he asked. "I was just out there fishing. I go fishing every Monday. Usually I bring home something for supper."

"We're not accusing you," Gage said. "But we're hoping you might have seen or heard something that could help us find the killer. Where were you between eight and ten this morning?"

"I was at the lake. I always try to get there by eight, and I leave about eleven to come home for lunch." He turned to Nate. "You saw me there. It must have been about nine or so when we talked."

Nate nodded. "That's about right. And you didn't see anyone else while you were at the lake?"

"Not a soul. I passed a couple of cars on the highway on my way out there, but once I turned onto the Forest Service Road, I didn't see any other cars, and none in the parking lot. I saw a woman out walking, but that was all."

Gage tensed. "A woman out walking? Where? What did she look like?"

"She was on the forest road, about a mile before the turnoff to the lake. She was tall and thin, with long blond hair—a lot of it."

"What was she doing?" Gage asked.

"Just walking along, talking on the phone. She didn't even look up when I passed."

"What else can you tell me about her?" Gage asked. "Did you recognize her?"

"She was wearing jeans and hiking boots and a black parka. I didn't get that good a look at her. She had her head bent, with that phone pressed to her ear and her hair falling all in her face."

"Had you ever seen her out there before?" Nate asked.

"No. I usually don't see anybody—not in the winter, anyway," Abel said. "I don't think there are any houses out that way."

"Didn't you think it was odd she was walking out there by herself?" Gage asked.

Abel shrugged. "People like to walk. It's none of my business. She didn't look like she was in trouble or anything. Just walking along, talking on the phone."

"What time was this that you saw her?" Gage asked.

"Well, it was before eight. Maybe seven fifty."

"Which direction was she walking?" Nate asked.

"North. Same direction I was headed."

They talked to him a few more minutes, but he couldn't tell them anything further. They said good-bye and returned to Gage's cruiser. Neither man spoke until they were headed back to the sheriff's department.

"The woman he saw wasn't Michaela," Gage said. "She has short, dark hair. And what was a woman doing out there by herself at that time of morning, anyway?"

"Something else really strange about that whole story," Nate said.

"I know what you're thinking," Gage said. "What was she doing on the phone?"

"Right. Jamie had to drive a ways to call in when she found Michaela. There's no phone signal out that way. None at all."

BANK PRESIDENT TOM BABCOCK met Travis and Jamie at the Mountain States Bank, a worried expression on his face. "I hope we can help you," he said as he led them past the teller windows to the back of the building. "It's unnerving to think a murderer is one of our customers."

"If he is a customer, it will make it easier for us to find him," Travis said.

"You said on the phone you wanted to see footage from our security cameras," Babcock said. "I've asked our IT specialist, Susan Whitmore, to meet with us. She knows her way around the system much better than I do." He opened the door to a small office filled with computer equipment. "While we wait for her, can you tell me a little more about this? You said our teller, Michaela Underwood, was murdered? And this man she met at the bank might be her killer?"

"We don't know that he killed her," Travis said. "But he was supposed to meet her this morning. It may be he knows something about what happened. Were you here on Thursday?"

"Yes. Michaela worked eight to five that day. She took lunch from eleven thirty to twelve thirty, and was the only teller on duty from twelve thirty to three."

"Do you remember her talking to a young man?" Travis asked. "Flirting with him?"

"I can't say that I noticed anything like that." He frowned. "Michaela was always very friendly. Customers liked her. We're going to really miss her. I can't imagine anyone wanting to hurt her..."

His voice trailed away as a chime sounded. "That will be Susan now." He leaned out of the open door. "We're back here, Susan," he called.

Susan Whitmore was a trim woman with very short platinum hair and piercing blue eyes. "Tom filled me in on the phone," she said after introductions were made. "Just tell me what you need, Sheriff, and I'll do my best to help."

"Michaela Underwood made a date to go snowshoeing this morning with a man she told her sister she met here at the bank Thursday," Travis explained. "He returned Friday and asked her out. We need to find this guy and talk to him. All we have is a first name—Al. If we can spot him talking to her on your security footage, we're hoping that will help us locate him."

"If you find him, we can look at the time stamp on the image and I can link him to a particular transaction," Tom said. "That should give you a name if he was cashing a check or making a deposit, or a payment on an account with us."

"Do you have a particular time you want to look at?" Susan asked. "Or the whole day?"

"Let's start with twelve thirty to three," Travis said. "When Michaela was the only teller working."

"All right." Susan inputted information into a computer and pulled up a black-and-white image showing four screens—ATM, front door, back door and a wider shot that took in most of the lobby. She clicked on the lobby view and enlarged it. "We'll start here, since this gives us a good view of Michaela. I'll scroll forward and stop on any male customers."

Jamie and Travis leaned in as Susan began to forward the film. Michaela waited on an older couple, a young woman with a child and two middle-aged women. Then a single man approached the counter. "Stop," Travis ordered.

Susan stilled the film. Jamie studied the image of a slender man, maybe six feet tall or just under. He wore a dark knit hat pulled down on his head, the collar of his dark coat turned up.

"Can you zoom in?" Travis asked.

Susan enlarged the image until it began to blur. Travis furrowed his brow. "Is there another camera, focused on the teller, which would give us a view of his face?" he asked.

"No," Susan said.

Travis sighed and stepped back. "The way he's standing, we can't tell anything about his face. We can't even tell whether his hair is light or dark."

"Do you think that's deliberate?" Jamie asked.

"Maybe," Travis said. "If he is the killer, he wouldn't want to be seen on video. The hat and coat do a good job of obscuring his face. He's wearing jeans and hiking boots."

"Maybe the brand of the boots will tell us something," Jamie said.

"We'll try," Travis said. He nodded to Susan. "Advance the tape again. Let's see what he does."

They had a clear view of Michaela, smiling and at one point even laughing, as the man stood in front of her. Then he left. But instead of turning to face the camera, he took a few steps back, still talking to Michaela. When he was almost out of reach of the camera, he whirled, head down, and hurried out of the frame.

"I'm willing to bet he knew about the security camera and didn't want to be seen," Travis said. "Let's see the footage for Friday."

But the footage from Friday yielded no sign of the

man. They spent almost an hour running through everything and saw no images of him. "Maybe she met him outside the bank," Jamie said. "On her lunch break or something."

"Maybe," Travis said. "It would be easy enough for him to wait for her in the parking lot or on the sidewalk and stop her before she went into the bank." He turned to Tom. "Did anything about him look familiar to you—like someone who had come into the bank before?"

Tom shook his head. "I'm sorry, no."

"What about the name Al? Does that make you think of anyone in particular?"

"I know an Allen and an Alvin, but both of them are in their fifties or sixties. And that wasn't them we saw on the video just now."

"I'm going to need all your security footage from the past week, including what we looked at today. It's possible this guy came in earlier, checking things out."

"Of course. Susan will get it for you."

"Can you tell us what kind of transaction he was making here Thursday?" Travis asked. "The time stamp on the security footage showed he walked up to the teller window at two sixteen."

Tom walked to a computer farther down the counter and began typing. A few moments later, he groaned. "Looks like it was a cash transaction."

"Such as?" Jamie asked.

"Breaking a large bill or cashing in rolled coins," Tom said.

"Here are the security discs for the time period you wanted." Susan handed Travis an envelope. Travis wrote out a receipt for her, then he and Jamie left.

"I got chills when Tom said it was a cash transaction," Jamie said when they were in Travis's cruiser. "Al had to know we couldn't trace that."

"Or maybe he was using the transaction as an excuse to hit on the cute teller," Travis said. He rubbed his hands along the steering wheel. "Not that I really believe that. I think we're on to something."

"This might be the killer." A shiver ran through Jamie as she said the words.

"Maybe." He shifted the cruiser into gear and began backing out of the parking spot. "In any case, this feels like the closest we've gotten."

NATE AND GAGE returned to the sheriff's department and waylaid Travis and Jamie as soon as they returned. "We got something from Abel Crutchfield that might be useful," Gage said as they followed Travis into his office. Jamie hung back, then followed, too, squeezing in to stand next to Nate. The soft, herbal scent of her hair made his heart race with a sudden memory of the two of them making out in the old Ford pickup he had driven at the time. Hastily, he shoved the memory away and focused on the conversation between the sheriff and his brother.

"Abel says he saw a woman—tall, thin, blonde—walking along Forest Service Road 1410 this morning," Gage said. "She was alone, no car around. He said he didn't get a real good look at her, because she had her head bent, talking on her phone."

"Except there isn't a phone signal out there," Nate said. "For any carrier."

"That does seem suspicious," Travis said.

Beside Nate, Jamie shifted. "Maybe it isn't really suspicious," she said.

She flushed when all three men turned to look at her but continued, her voice even. "Maybe she was nervous, being out there alone. She heard the guy's truck and pulled out her phone and pretended to be talking to someone so whoever was driving past would get the idea she could summon help if she needed to."

"Do women really do things like that?" Nate asked and wished he could take the words back as soon as he said them.

"Yeah, they do," she said, the expression in her eyes making him feel about three feet tall. "Because you know—men."

None of them had a good response to this. The silence stretched. Finally, Travis said, "Let's see if we can find anyone else who saw this woman. I also have a list of bank employees. Let's talk to them and see if any of them remember 'Al.' Jamie, I want you to help with that. Most of the employees are young women—they might be more willing to open up to you." He clicked a few keys on his laptop. "I just forwarded the list to you."

"I'll get right on it," she said, then slipped out the door.

"I'll see if I can find any campers or snowshoers or skiers or fishermen who might have seen a woman who fits the description Abel gave us," Nate said.

"Let's not drop the ball on his," Travis said.

"Right," Nate said. He wasn't going to drop the ball on Jamie, either. He'd do whatever it took to make her see he wasn't the boy who had hurt her seven years ago. She might never feel close to him again, but at least they could be friends.

Chapter Five

Jamie left the sheriff's department at nine o'clock, after working her way through half the bank employees on the list Travis had forwarded to her. So far, none of the people she'd spoken to remembered Michaela talking to anyone special, and they had no recollection of a single man who stood out for them.

She picked up a sleepy Donna from Mrs. Simmons's house. Donna had already taken a bath and changed into a pair of flannel pajamas with large, colorful dogs all over them. Jamie had a pair just like them. Over the past couple of years, Donna had gotten into the habit of keeping a number of clothes at the caregiver's house, which made things easier for everyone. As Jamie put an arm around Donna and escorted her into their house, she caught the smell of the coconut shampoo her sister used. The scent and the feel of the soft flannel beneath her hand transported her back to the days when Donna was little and Jamie, seven years older, often helped her get ready for bed. Once Donna was bathed and dressed in pajamas, the sisters would snuggle together in Donna's bed, and Jamie would read to her until she fell asleep.

Tonight, she led her upstairs to the room across the hall from Jamie's own and tucked her in. Donna turned on her side and studied the big whiteboard on her bedroom wall, where Jamie drew in a calendar every month and noted both sisters' schedules. Donna liked knowing what was supposed to happen each day. "Work tomorrow," she said. "I'll see Henry."

Right, Jamie thought as she kissed her sister, then switched out the light. Sometime tomorrow she'd have to find time to stop by the grocery store and check out Henry. He was probably harmless, but it didn't hurt to be careful.

She walked across the hall to her room and exchanged her uniform for yoga pants and an oversize sweatshirt. Taking off the heavy utility belt and body armor was the definite signal that she was off duty Time to relax. Except she was too restless to settle. She went downstairs and wandered through the familiar rooms the kitchen, with its white-painted cabinets and blue Formica countertops; the formal dining room she had turned into a home office; and the wood-paneled living room with its comfortable tweed-covered sofa and chairs and heavy wood tables. The house was out of style but comfortable and familiar.

She and Donna had grown up in this house and had lived here together until Jamie had gone off to college. She hadn't gone far—only across the mountains to Boulder, and the University of Colorado. She had studied business, thinking she would look for a job in Junction, so that she could be close to Donna and her parents. Then, her parents had been killed in a car accident, plowed into by a tourist who was texting while driving. The tourist had walked away with only a few bruises, while her parents had both been pronounced dead at the scene.

So much for a business career in Junction. Jamie needed to be in Eagle Mountain, with Donna. She might have sold the family home and moved with her sister to Junction or Denver or somewhere else, but the thought made her heart ache. Eagle Mountain was home. And Donna didn't do well with change. She needed familiar things—her home, the neighbors she knew, her job at the grocery store—to keep her firmly grounded.

Jamie had moved back to Eagle Mountain for good four years ago. After a series of low-paying clerical jobs, the opportunity at the sheriff's department had been a welcome relief—a way for Jamie to stay in Eagle Mountain and earn a living that would support her and her sister. But it had also been a lifesaver because it gave Jamie a focus and purpose. She had discovered, somewhat to her surprise, that she loved the work. She liked looking out for her hometown and the people in it, and she liked being part of a team that was trying to protect everyone here.

Oh, it wasn't all good feelings and easy times. She had been sworn at by people she stopped for traffic violations, kicked and punched by a shoplifter she had chased down on Main Street, with half a dozen locals and tourists standing around watching the battle and no one lifting a finger to help her. And she had looked on the bodies of those murdered women and felt a mixture of sickness and anger—and a fierce desire to stop the man before he hurt anyone else.

The loud trill of an old-fashioned phone startled her. She raced to grab her cell phone off the hall table, and frowned at the screen, which showed Unknown Number. A sales call? A scammer? Or maybe one of the bank employees, calling her back because he or she had remembered something. She answered, cautious. "Hello?"

"It's Nate. I called to see how you're doing."

The deep voice vibrated through her, making her heart flutter, but she steeled herself against the sensation. The question—coming from him—annoyed her. "I'm fine. Why wouldn't I be?"

"Finding a dead woman shakes up most people. It shook me up."

She settled onto the sofa, a pillow hugged to her stomach. "I'm fine," she said. "It's part of the job. I knew that going in."

"From what I saw today, you're good at your job."

Was he flattering her, trying to persuade her to forgive him? She sighed. "Nate, I don't want to do this."

"Do what?"

"I don't want to pretend we're friends. We're not. We can't be."

"Why not?"

"You know why not."

A long pause. She began to wonder if he had hung

up on her. Then he said. "So, because we were once lovers—each other's first lovers—we can't be friends now? Jamie, that was seven years ago. We were kids."

"And now we're adults, and we don't have to pretend we're two old pals."

"I don't know why not," he said. "There was a time I knew you better than anyone—and you knew me better."

"Like you said, that was seven years ago." A lot had happened since then. She wasn't the same woman anymore.

"We're going to be working together on this case," he said. "We shouldn't be enemies."

"You're not my enemy." Did he really think that? "But we can't be…close…anymore."

"Why not?"

Because if she let him too close, she knew she would fall for him again. And she couldn't trust him to not leave her again—at the next promotion, or if someone better came along. He had proved before that he looked out for his own interests and he wasn't one to stick with a relationship if things got tough. "It would be too complicated," she said. "I know you don't like that." He had said that when he broke up with her before. *There's no sense us staying together. It would be too complicated.*

Was that sound him grinding his teeth together? "You've got a lot of wrong ideas about me," he said.

"You're the one who gave them to me."

"Fine. Have it your way. We won't be 'close'—

whatever that means to you. But we can be civil. Don't make this more difficult than it has to be."

"I wouldn't dream of it. Now I'd better go. We'll have another long day tomorrow. Good night."

She didn't wait for him to answer but hung up. She'd handled that well, she thought. No sense starting something that was bound to end badly. She'd been very mature and matter-of-fact. She ought to be proud of herself.

She knew a lot about grief now. The pain never went away, but with time, it always got better.

NATE SCANNED THE sheltered meadow at the base of Mount Wilson with his binoculars, counting the number of elk in the small herd gathered there. Most of them still looked to be in good shape, but this would be a good place to put one of the feeding stations the Department of Wildlife had decided to set up starting this weekend. Local ranchers and hunters had volunteered to help distribute the hay and pellets to the three main feeding sites in the area. The supplies were being delivered by helicopter, which meant the project wouldn't be hampered by the still-closed highway.

He entered the information about the herd into a database on his phone, then snowshoed back to the trailhead where he had left his truck. Once inside the cab, with the heater turned up high, he headed down the road, his speed at a crawl, alert for signs of anything unusual. As he passed the turnout toward a closed campground, he caught a flash of color through the trees and stopped. The binoculars came out and he zeroed in on a dark gray SUV parked up against an icy expanse of exposed rock. He scanned the area and focused in on two climbers halfway up the ice.

He followed the SUV's tracks in the snow and parked behind the vehicle. By the time he got out of his truck, the two climbers were headed down. He walked over and met them when their feet hit the snow. No helmets, he noted, and no ropes or harnesses or other safety gear. Maybe they thought they didn't need it, that their spiked shoes and ice axes were enough.

The first man, about six feet tall, with a slight build and sandy hair cut short, eyed Nate suspiciously. "You need something?" he asked.

"You and your friend climb here often?" Nate asked as the other young man, who was a couple of inches taller than his companion and had a head of brown curls, joined them. Something about these two was familiar, but he couldn't place them. Maybe he had seen them around town somewhere.

"Sometimes," the first man said. "There's no law against it." He ran his thumb along the edge of the ice ax he hefted. It wasn't a threatening gesture, but it made Nate aware of the ax as a weapon.

"No, there's not." He addressed the second young man, who also had an ice ax, which he held down by his side. "Were the two of you around here yesterday?"

"Not yesterday," the dark-haired man said. "Why do you want to know?"

"I'm looking for anyone who might have seen a

blonde woman in this area, alone, yesterday morning," Nate said. "What are your names?"

"I'm Lex." The blond offered his hand, and gave a firm shake. "This is Ty."

"Did the two of you see a woman around here yesterday morning—blond hair, walking alongside the road?"

The barest flicker of a glance passed between the two climbers. "We weren't here yesterday," Lex said.

"Right," Nate said. "What about the other times you've been out here? Have you ever seen a woman like that in this area?"

A longer exchange of glances, then Ty shook his head. "No. We've run into women climbing at the park in town but not out here."

"I wouldn't think any woman would risk walking along the road by herself around here," Lex said. "Not with that serial killer going around offing women." His expression became more animated. "Somebody at the restaurant last night said something about another woman being killed yesterday. Was this blonde the Ice Cold Killer's latest victim?"

"No," Nate said. "The sheriff would just like to talk to her."

"This guy's sure making the sheriff look like an idiot," Lex said. "Killing all these women practically under his nose."

"I heard one of the victims was even done in on the sheriff's family ranch," Ty said. "That's got to have him furious."

"The sheriff definitely isn't an idiot," Nate said.

"Have you seen anyone else in the area—fishermen, hikers, other climbers? It's possible one of them was here yesterday and saw this woman."

"We see people all the time," Ty said. "But most of them we never know their names."

"You're kind of grasping at straws, aren't you?" Lex asked. "Questioning random people in the woods isn't going to help you find this killer."

Three years on the job had given Nate plenty of experience dealing with the public. He'd gotten into the habit of identifying them as particular types. He'd learned to deal with each type a different way. Nate cataloged these two as civilian know-it-alls, always happy to tell him how to do his job. "Do either of you know a guy named Al?" he asked.

Lex laughed. "There was a guy named Al in my organic chemistry class last semester. Do you think he's your killer?"

"Have you met anyone named Al in Eagle Mountain?" Nate asked.

"Nope," Ty said. "But then, we don't know many people here."

"So you're students?"

"Graduated," Lex said.

"What do you do now?" Nate asked.

"Right now, we're going to try another route up this ice." He turned back toward the rock face. "Good luck with your search."

Not waiting for Nate to say anything else, Lex stepped up onto a small protrusion in the ice, swung his ax over his head and buried the tip with a heavy

thud. Ty moved ten feet farther down the face and began to climb also. Nate might not even have been there, for all they were concerned.

Their disdain grated, but Nate knew he was better off ignoring them the same way they ignored him. They didn't have anything to tell him. But he made note of the license tag on their SUV as he walked back to his truck. When he had a better cell signal, he'd call it in.

From there, he drove past the spot where they had found Michaela in her car. Crime scene tape still festooned the area, and someone had left a bouquet of flowers in the snow on the shoulder of the road, the blossoms of what might have been daisies and carnations wilting and turning brown in the cold.

He passed the parking area for the snowshoe trail and thought of Jamie, and the anger with which she had confronted him yesterday. He was aware she had been cool to him since his return to Eagle Mountain, but her coldness had surprised him. Her initial agitation over her runaway dogs had morphed into real ire—almost as if she was continuing the last conversation they had had, like it was the next day instead of seven years later. At one time, her reaction might have caused him to respond in anger, also. Now, with time and maturity, the fact that she still had such strong feelings intrigued him.

Jamie had been his best friend at one time, the one person in the world he knew he could always count on. Things had ended badly between them—and he was willing to take his share of responsibility for

that. But life was too short to throw away a friend-
ship like that.

He was close enough now to a group of private
summer cabins that he decided to go a little out of
his way and check them out. Though not strictly part
of his duties, he liked to do a regular drive-by of the
properties, to check for any vandalism, break-ins or
maintenance issues. The cabins, a cluster of seven log
structures of one or two rooms each, were privately
owned, but on Forest Service land. Most of the cabins
had been built eighty or a hundred years ago and the
owners were allowed to continue to use them after
the land was turned over to the Forest Service. They
weren't allowed to enlarge the cabins or use them for
any other purpose. Most of them weren't suitable for
year-round living, anyway, being uninsulated and off-
grid, and Nate had yet to encounter anyone out here
after the first snow.

He turned onto the road leading up to the cabins
and parked in front of the heavy chain that blocked
the way. Half a dozen heavy locks hung from the
chain. Cabin owners or friends would have combi-
nations or keys that allowed them to open the chain
and pass through. Nate studied the obviously fresh
tire tracks on either side of the chain. Someone had
entered and exited this way in the last day or so—
maybe even this morning. Possibly one of the cabin
owners had stopped by to check on his property.

Leaving his truck parked, Nate stepped over the
chain and followed a winding track to the first cabin.
Old wooden shutters covered the windows of the

structure—protection against weather and both four-legged and two-legged animals. A hand-painted sign hung over the door, *Lazy Daze* burned into the wood.

Nate followed the tire tracks past four more cabins, all the way back to the most remote in the grouping, set a short distance from the others. No one was at the cabin now, but tracks in the snow showed where a vehicle had parked, and where at least two people had walked around. Like the first cabin, wooden shutters covered the windows and the door was padlocked. Nate studied the door, unable to shake the uneasiness that had his nerves on hyperalert. Something wasn't right here. He sniffed the air and caught the sharp tang of wood smoke, and shifted his gaze to the chimney of the cabin. No smoke emanated from it now, but someone might have had a fire in there recently.

He walked around the side of the cabin, hoping to find an uncovered window that would allow him to peek in. He spotted a door that provided access to a covered back porch and headed for it, intending to check if it was locked. But he hadn't gone far when something clamped onto his ankle, pain lancing through him, stealing his breath. Vision fogged with shock, he stared down at the jagged steel trap clamped around his foot.

Chapter Six

"We've had a garbled radio transmission from one of our officers." The woman from Colorado Parks and Wildlife who contacted dispatch spoke with a distinct Texas drawl. "All of the personnel in this area are involved in the supply delivery near County Road Two. I didn't get a reply when I tried to make contact again, but reception is very bad in that area. Could one of your officers check it out for us?"

"I can take that," Jamie said. "I'm headed out now." She had stopped by the dispatch center to say hello to her friend, Anong, who was on duty that afternoon.

Anong keyed her microphone. "I have a deputy here who can check out that call for you," she said. "What is the location?"

"We think it came from somewhere around Sundance cabins—the summer cabins off Forest Service Road 1410? Wildlife officer Nate Hall."

Jamie bit back a groan of annoyance. Was this some twisted way for Nate to make sure he saw her again? But she immediately dismissed that notion, and a tickle of fear replaced her irritation. Was Nate in some kind of trouble? "I'm on my way," she said.

"I'll let the sheriff's department know what's up," Anong said, her wide face soft with concern. "Is Officer Hall a friend of yours?"

"Not exactly."

Nate wasn't a friend, but he wasn't her enemy. She had meant that. And even if she had hated his guts, he was a fellow officer who might be in trouble. She was in her cruiser headed out of town when the sheriff called her. "I'm sending Gage out as backup," he said.

"Nate's going to be really embarrassed if this is the radio equivalent of a butt dial," she said.

"Better embarrassed than in real trouble," Travis said.

"Yes, sir."

She punched the accelerator, going as fast as she dared on the icy roads. She resisted the urge to switch on her lights and sirens. That was a sure way to draw a crowd. She wouldn't mind embarrassing Nate a little but no need to go overboard. And if he was in a dangerous situation, no sense putting other people at risk.

She spotted his truck parked at the entrance to the enclave of summer cabins. The chain over the road was in place, and nothing looked out of order. She got out of her cruiser and spotted tire tracks leading toward the cabins. Had Nate seen someone and followed them—or was he merely checking the cabins for signs of vandalism or break-ins? It was something they had had trouble with in the past—usually bored teens breaking into a cabin to have a party or mess things up.

She cupped her hands around her mouth. "Nate!"

Her voice echoed back to her, followed by ringing silence. A chill wind buffeted her, and she rubbed her shoulders against the cold. Better to get back in the cruiser and wait for Gage to arrive. She turned back toward her vehicle, then froze as a cry reached her—an animal sound that sent an icy jolt through her. Heart hammering, she raced toward the sound. "Nate!" she shouted again.

The reply was stronger now, a strangled cry for help. She ran faster, slipping and falling on the ice, but picking herself up and charging on. She found him alongside a cabin, hunched over on the ground, his face as pale as the snow around him. "Jamie!"

"Nate, what happened?" She fell to her knees beside him, then recoiled in horror at the sight of the trap around his foot. The steel teeth had sliced through his thick pack boots and blood stained the snow around him. She swallowed hard. "Who would have something like that out here?"

"I think it was a booby trap," he said. "It was covered up pretty well, and it's attached to the cabin, so that anyone caught in it couldn't get away." He indicated the thick chain that ran between the trap and the cabin wall, where it was fastened to an iron ring sunk into one of the logs.

She forced herself to ignore the blood and her thoughts of what the trap must have done to Nate's leg, and bent to study the contraption itself. Then she grasped the sides of the trap and pulled hard, but barely managed to move them. "You can't open it that way," Nate said. "You have to stand on it. See these pieces?" He indicated ear-shaped metal pieces on either side of the trap's jaw. "Stand on them and your weight will force the trap open."

"All right." She stood and he scooted back, giving her room to position herself. She straddled the trap, facing him. "I don't want to hurt you," she said.

"It already hurts like the devil," he said. "You can't make it worse. Just do it and get it over with."

Right. She took a deep breath, then stepped down on first one ear, then the other. The jaws eased open. With a groan, Nate pulled his foot from the trap. Jamie shoved the trap aside and knelt beside him once more. "I should go call an ambulance," she said. "Will you be okay if I leave you?"

"I kept waiting for whoever did this to come back." He lifted a pistol from the ground beside him. "But they didn't show." He frowned. "How did you know I was here?"

"Someone from your office called and said they had had a garbled transmission from you and asked us to check it out."

"And you were the lucky one." His eyes met hers. She wanted to look away but couldn't, mesmerized by the tenderness behind the pain. She remembered other times when he had looked in her eyes that way, moments when they had trusted each other with secrets, turned to each other for comfort or united in lovemaking. She leaned toward him, drawn by the pull of memories and a longing she hadn't even realized was in her, to feel that close again.

"Jamie! Nate! What's going on?"

Gage's shouts yanked her back to the present and she pulled away, then stood and went to meet him. "Someone set a leghold trap beside this cabin and Nate stepped in it," she said.

Gage followed her to where Nate sat. He had dragged himself over to lean against the wall of the cabin, a thin trail of blood marking his path. "How are you doing?" Gage asked.

"The bleeding has almost stopped. My boot is ruined, but it probably kept the trap from destroying my leg." He grimaced at his mangled boot. "The ankle might be fractured, but it's not a bad break. It doesn't hurt as much, now that the pressure of the trap is off."

Gage squatted down to get a better look at the trap. "I hope you're up on your tetanus shots," he said. "This thing is pretty rusty."

"It's an old trap," Nate said. "An antique. New ones have smooth jaws, not toothed ones. I seem to remember one of these cabins had some old traps hanging up on the wall. Not this one, but another in this group. Take a look for me, will you?"

"I will, after we get an ambulance for you," Gage said.

"I don't need an ambulance," Nate said. "The two of you can get me to one of your vehicles. That will be a lot faster than waiting for an ambulance to come all the way out here—especially since you'll have to drive halfway back to town to get a cell signal."

Gage studied him a moment, then nodded. "All right. I guess we could do that." He looked around them. "What about whoever did this?"

"I'd like to get a look inside this cabin," Nate said. "The tracks in the snow indicate someone has been here recently. Maybe someone is squatting here and they set the trap to discourage anyone investigating too closely."

"Then they're not very bright," Gage said. "They had to know someone getting hurt in a trap like that would bring the law down on this place."

"Maybe they thought they could get to whoever was caught before anyone else found out," Nate said.

"We'll get someone out here to take a look," Gage said. "First, let's get you to the clinic in town." He offered his hand and Nate grasped it and heaved to his feet.

Jamie rushed in to steady him, and Gage moved in on the other side. "We could make a chair and carry you," Gage said.

"I've still got one good leg," Nate said. "I might as well use it."

Slowly, awkwardly, they made their way around the cabin and onto the road. Nate gritted his teeth and breathed hard but made no protest. After what seemed like an hour—but was probably only fifteen minutes—they reached Jamie's cruiser. Gage opened the door and helped Nate into the passenger seat. "You take him to the clinic," Gage said. "I'll stay here and make sure no one disturbs the crime scene. You phone for help when you get into cell range."

"All right."

Nate said nothing on the drive into town. Eyes closed, he rested his head against the window. Jamie wondered if he was asleep. When they reached the turnoff onto the county road, Jamie called Adelaide and told her what had happened. She promised to call ahead to the clinic and to send Dwight and another deputy to assist Gage.

Jamie ended the call and looked at Nate. His eyes were open and he was watching her. "You okay?" she asked, focusing on the road again.

"I'm okay."

At the clinic, Jamie insisted on fetching a wheelchair from inside to transport Nate inside. He didn't object. When questioned by the staff about how he ended up with his leg caught in a trap, he said, "I'm a wildlife officer," as if that explained everything.

X-rays revealed his ankle was badly bruised, the skin mangled and requiring stitches, but it wasn't broken. "Those pack boots have a lot of padding," the doctor said as Nate completed the final paperwork for his visit. "That probably saved you."

He left with his ankle in an air splint, hobbling on crutches. "I'll drive you home," Jamie said.

He directed her to a cabin on a ranch on the edge of town. "The original owner built it as an artist's studio," Nate said as he unlocked the door. "Come in and take a look."

She moved past him, into a room with blond wood floors and large windows that flooded the space with natural light. A galley kitchen filled the corner of the room, and doors opened onto a single bedroom and bath. "How did you ever find this place?" she asked, not hiding her admiration.

Nate sank onto the leather sofa and leaned the crutches against the wall behind him. "The officer who had my job before me lived here," he said. "When he moved to Cortez, he worked out a deal with the landlord for me to take over his lease."

It felt awkward standing while he was sitting, so she sat on the other end of the sofa. "I guess your parents don't still have a place in town, do they?" she asked.

"No, they sold out and moved to Texas three years ago. My dad said he got tired of shoveling snow, and my brother and his kids are in Dallas and my mom wanted to be closer to the grandkids."

"I guess I lost track of them," she said. "I had a lot going on just then."

"Your parents' deaths," he said. "I remember. My mom told me." He leaned over and fiddled with the fastening on his Aircast. "I kept meaning to get in touch with you, to tell you how sorry I was." He glanced at her. "I guess I messed that up, too."

She shook her head. "It's all right." She had been so devastated at the time she couldn't even remember who had or hadn't expressed their sympathy.

"That must have been rough," he said. "Losing both of them at once. Mom said you were living in Boulder at the time."

"Yeah. I came home to take care of Donna. She

was so upset. It took her a long time before she could accept that they weren't coming back."

"You could have taken her with you, gone back to the city."

"I didn't want to do that to her. She had already lost her parents—I couldn't have her lose her home and her friends, all the things that were familiar to her. Routine is really important to her."

"What about all you lost?" he said. "You must have had a job, friends, a home?"

She shifted to angle her body toward him. "Eagle Mountain is my home. And I had just graduated. It's not as if I had a career or anything. Besides, if I hadn't come back here, I never would have gotten into law enforcement. I'd have probably ended up in a cubicle somewhere, bored out of my mind, instead of doing something active that I'm good at. Besides, who are you to give me a hard time about coming back here to live? You did it."

"Yeah, I did. It was a good opportunity for me." He shrugged. "And I missed it. I missed a lot of things." His gaze zeroed in on her.

She stood. "I'd better go. Somebody will return your truck tomorrow, I imagine."

Before he could protest, his phone rang. She headed for the door. He answered the call and said, "Wait up a minute. It's Gage."

Hand on the doorknob, she paused. Nate listened a moment, then said, "Jamie is here. I'm going to put you on speaker. Tell her what you told me."

"We found evidence that someone was squatting

in that cabin," Gage said. "Maybe more than one person. We've got a reserve deputy sitting on the place waiting for them to come back. We'll want to question them about that trap. How's the leg?"

"Bad bruise, no break, some stitches," Nate said. "I have to stay off it a few days."

"You got lucky," Gage said.

"I guess you could look at it that way."

"We found two more of those traps—one on the other side of the cabin, and one near the front steps," Gage said. "Looks like you missed that second one by inches, judging by your prints in the snow. And you were right—the traps were taken off the wall of a nearby cabin."

"Is there anything in the cabin to tell you the identity of the squatter?"

"Not much—some blankets, dishes, canned food. We talked to the owner—he lives in Nebraska—and it sounds like everything we found was stuff that he keeps there."

"How did the squatter get in? I didn't see any sign of a break-in."

"The owner keeps the key under a flowerpot on the back porch. It's not there now."

Nate rolled his eyes. "Well, it'll be interesting to see if anyone shows up and who they are."

"I'm wondering if it might be our killer," Gage said.

"What makes you think that?" Nate asked.

"Just a hunch. I mean, if you wanted to stay off the radar, this would be a good place to hide, wouldn't it?"

Chapter Seven

"Henry and I have a date!" Donna announced at breakfast the next morning. Sunlight streamed from the window behind her, promising another beautiful day.

"Oh?" Jamie tried not to show too much curiosity. She still hadn't gotten by the store to meet Henry, though she needed to do so soon.

"He's going to take me to dinner and the movies." Donna spoke around a mouthful of half-chewed cereal.

"Don't talk with your mouth full," Jamie chided. "And we don't have a movie theatre in Eagle Mountain."

Donna chewed and swallowed. "I know that," she said. "We're going to watch a movie at his house."

"When are you planning to do this?"

"Soon."

Which could mean next month or this afternoon. "You can't go out with Henry until I meet him," Jamie said.

"Why do you have to meet him? He's *my* boyfriend."

"I still need to check him out and make sure he's a good person for you to date." That he wasn't someone who was trying to take advantage of Donna's vulnerability.

"I don't have to approve of your boyfriends."

"I don't have any boyfriends." She had had only a few casual dates since breaking up with Nate. Thinking about that now made her feel pathetic. But she was far too busy to have time for a relationship.

"But if you did, you wouldn't wait for my permission to date them," Donna said. "I shouldn't have to, either."

"I'm your big sister. It's my job to look after you."

"I'm nineteen. I don't need you to look after me."

But you do, Jamie thought. Donna knew it, too, even if she wouldn't admit it. Jamie could understand that her sister was frustrated that she wasn't able to do the things other people her age could do. She was high-functioning, but she had led a sheltered life. She didn't understand that there were people in the world who would take advantage of her. "I'm not saying you can't go out with Henry," she said. "I just want to meet him first." She leaned across the table and put her hand over Donna's. "I would say that even if we switched places and you were just like me." The words weren't a lie. If Michaela's family had insisted on meeting "Al" before Michaela went out with him, maybe the bank teller would be alive today.

But Donna was in a stubborn mood this morning. "What if I don't want you to meet him?"

"Donna, please. If he's your friend, of course I want to meet him."

"He's *my* friend. Can't I have anything that's just mine?" She shoved back her chair and stomped off.

Jamie sighed and resisted the urge to get up and follow Donna. It wouldn't hurt to let her sulk a little. And her bad moods rarely lasted long.

Ten minutes later, after Jamie had finished breakfast and cleared away the dishes, she found Donna waiting by the front door, her backpack in hand. "Time to go to work," she said.

"It is," Jamie said. "When you get off at three, you know to come straight to Mrs. Simmons's?"

"I know." She headed out the door to Jamie's cruiser.

The two sisters didn't speak on the short drive to the grocery store. Donna could walk the few blocks from their house to the store, but Jamie liked to drive her when she could. "Is Henry working today?" she asked as she pulled into the parking lot.

"He is." Donna opened the door. "'Bye." She hurried into the store, not looking back.

Jamie made a note to swing by later and find out exactly when Henry would be working, as well as his last name and more about him.

She parked behind the sheriff's department and entered through the back door. Adelaide waylaid her as she emerged from the locked room. "We're holding a masquerade ball at the community center Friday night, all proceeds to benefit folks in town for whom the road closures have caused a financial hardship. I hope you plan to be there."

"Oh." Jamie blinked. "A masquerade party?"

"Wear a costume and a mask." Adelaide looked her up and down. "I'm sure you're creative enough to come up with something. If you can't, the volunteers at the Humane Society thrift store have combed through donations and assembled a number of suitable disguises at very reasonable prices. And you're not on schedule to work that evening—I already checked."

"I don't know." Jamie searched for some excuse, but it was tough to think straight with Adelaide's steel gaze boring into her. Seventy-plus years, much of it spent bossing people around, had made the sheriff's department office manager a formidable force.

"It's for a good cause," Adelaide said. "People who work on the other side of the pass haven't been able to get to work, and store owners have suffered losses with fewer tourists visiting and the inability to replenish their stocks. People are really hurting and we want to help them."

"Of course," Jamie said. "I'll be there." Maybe she'd take Donna. Her sister liked dressing up, and she would enjoy seeing everyone's costumes.

Satisfied, Adelaide let her pass. Jamie made her way to the conference room, helped herself to a cup of coffee but bypassed the box of doughnuts. She settled at the table next to Dwight. A few moments later Nate clumped in on crutches and sank into the chair across from her. He looked better than he had yesterday. "How's the ankle?" she asked.

"It's there."

The sheriff entered the room and they all settled in to listen to the usual bulletins and updates, including a summary of the previous day's events at the summer cabins, for anyone who might not have gotten the full story yet. "No one showed up at the cabin while our officer was there," Travis said. "We can't afford to post someone there full-time, but if any of you are in the area, make it a point to swing by." He glanced down at his open laptop. "Did we get anything from Michaela Underwood's phone records?"

"There was one call at eight oh two the morning she was killed," Dwight said. "That could have been from Al. It came from a payphone at the Shell station. It's probably the only payphone in town. The phone box is around the side of the building, out of view of the road, and no one remembers seeing anyone using it that morning."

"Where are we on the search for the blonde woman Abel Crutchfield saw walking along Forest Service Road 1410?" Travis asked.

"Nowhere," Gage said. "We haven't found anyone else who saw her, or any blonde woman who lives out that way. In fact, no one lives out that way."

"What about the bank employees?" Travis asked.

"I interviewed all the employees," Jamie said. She checked her notes. "One woman, Janis Endicott, remembers Michaela talking about Al, but none of them remember seeing him or could give any new details."

"Anything else on this case?" Travis asked. "Any thoughts or insights any of you might have had about it?"

"I thought of one thing," Jamie said. When every head swiveled to look at her, she fought down a blush and forced herself to keep her voice steady. "While the other women who were killed seemed like crimes of opportunity, he apparently targeted Michaela."

"We could be dealing with a copycat," Dwight said.

"Maybe," Travis said. "Though nothing we've learned about Michaela points to her having an enemy who would want to kill her. And we can't be sure our killer didn't target and stalk any of the other women." He turned to Jamie. "That's good thinking, Deputy."

She swallowed, steeling herself for her next words. "I also thought maybe we should give the killer a target and see if he takes the bait."

"What are you talking about?" Nate hadn't said anything so far in the meeting, but he spoke up now.

Jamie shifted in her chair. She had lain awake a long time last night, thinking about this. "I could drive around, out of uniform and in my personal vehicle, in some of the areas we know he's killed other women and see if anyone behaves suspiciously."

"No." Nate spoke loudly and leaned across the table toward her.

She shrank back. "I'd be smart," she said. "And we could have other officers watching me."

"It might not be a bad idea," Travis said. "You

wouldn't have to be alone. We could have another officer hidden in the car with you."

Nate leaned back in his chair, silent, though he continued to glare at Jamie. She ignored him. "I think it's worth a try," she said.

Travis nodded. "I think so, too. We'll set something up for this evening. Dwight, you can go with her."

"Yes, sir."

Jamie struggled to remain composed, even as an adrenaline rush at the thought of possibly facing down a killer—or helping to capture him—made it difficult to sit still.

The rest of the meeting was a blur of routine announcements about training, schedules and upcoming events—including the masquerade party on Friday. When the sheriff dismissed them, she rose and left the room, intending to head out on patrol. Nate followed on her heels. "Jamie, wait up."

She stopped and looked back at him as he limped down the hallway toward her. "If you're going to lecture me about how I shouldn't put myself out there as bait for a killer, don't waste your breath," she said. "I'll be perfectly safe."

"More like it will all be a waste of time," he said. "I think this guy is too smart to fall for a trap like that."

"It's worth a try," she said.

He nodded. "I wish I could go with you."

She looked down at the cast on his foot. "I suppose you could bash the killer over the head with your crutches."

He laughed. "Yeah, well, just be careful."

"I'm always careful," she said.

"Yeah, you are, aren't you?"

How was she supposed to interpret the look he gave her? Equal parts frustration and—was that pity? She shook her head. She was imagining things. Nate might still have a few feelings for the girl she had been, but he didn't know enough about her now to really care.

"OFFICER HALL, AREN'T you supposed to be home, resting?"

Nate did his best to stand up straight—despite his cast and crutches—as he swiveled to face Adelaide. The septuagenarian eyed him over the top of purple-framed bifocals, her gaze taking in his khaki uniform. "Surely you aren't on duty?"

"I came in to give the sheriff my formal statement about what happened yesterday," Nate said. "And I'm in uniform because I'm here in an official capacity, as an officer of Parks and Wildlife." That was what he had told himself, anyway. It didn't feel right to show up at the sheriff's department in civilian clothing. Whether it was the uniform or the sheriff feeling sorry for him, Travis had asked Nate to sit in on the morning meeting.

"How long are you going to be laid up with your injuries?" Adelaide asked.

"Six weeks. Maybe less." He was determined to get back to work as swiftly as possible. The idea of sitting around the house with his foot up for the next month and a half was beyond depressing.

"If you're determined to be up and about so soon, you should come to the masquerade ball this Friday night." Adelaide handed him a postcard. The front of the card showed an attractive woman with a black, feathered mask hiding her features. "Proceeds benefit the folks here in Eagle Mountain who have been hit hardest by the heavy snow and road closures. There will be food, music and dancing, and prizes for the best costumes."

"I don't think I'll be doing any dancing just yet," Nate said. He tried to hand the card back to Adelaide, but she refused to take it.

"You can sit, have a drink and something to eat, and enjoy seeing everyone's costumes."

"What are you coming as?" he asked Adelaide.

The devilish look that came into her fading blue eyes made him take a step back. "You'll just have to wait and see. One more reason for you to show up."

"I'll, uh, think about it." He retreated to the door, moving faster than he would have thought possible in his condition.

His next stop was the grocery store. If he was going to be sitting home for the next few weeks, he needed to stock up on snacks and easy meals. He made his way to the produce section and was sizing up the potatoes when a familiar voice hailed him. "Hello, Officer Nate."

Smiling, he turned to greet Donna Douglas. Jamie's sister wore one of the grocery's blue aprons over a green sweater and jeans, her curly brown hair pulled back in a ponytail. He had never paid much attention to her when he and Jamie were dating. He'd thought of her as just a kid, seeming younger than her years because of her mental disability. "Hello, Donna," he said.

"You're Jamie's friend." Donna grinned. "Her boyfriend."

How was he supposed to answer that? "Jamie and I are friends."

"What happened to your foot?" She stared at the blue Aircast encasing his left foot.

"I hurt it at work."

"What kind of work do you do?"

"I work for Parks and Wildlife."

"I remember now. We met you when we were snowshoeing. Did a big animal step on your foot?"

"Not exactly."

"Hey, Donna."

They turned to see a stocky, moon-faced young man wheeling a produce cart toward them. His blue eyes shone from behind his black-framed glasses as he grinned at Donna. Donna grinned back. It made Nate think of cartoons he had seen as a child, where a pair of lovers looked at each other and hearts exploded in the air around them. He couldn't see any hearts around these two, but he had no doubt they were there.

"This is Henry." Donna took the young man's hand when he stopped beside them. "He's my boyfriend."

Henry nodded. "Donna's my girlfriend."

"You look like you make a good couple," Nate said.

"Thanks." Donna released Henry's hand. "I have to get back to work," she said. "We don't want to get in trouble." She waved to Nate and hurried back toward the register area.

"Me, too," Henry said. He began unloading apples from a box on a cart, arranging them in a neat pyramid. "You should buy an apple." He handed Nate a large red fruit. "They're very good, and good for you."

"I think I will." Nate pulled a plastic bag from the roll at one end of the bin and selected three more apples to go with the one Henry had given him.

"Are you a police officer?" Henry was staring at Nate's khaki uniform and gun.

"A kind of police officer, yes." He didn't mention Parks and Wildlife. When he named his employer, people invariably thought he was a park ranger, not a cop. Never mind that he had the same training as any other law enforcement officer. He wrote tickets, investigated crimes and made arrests all the time as part of his job. And most of the lawbreakers he faced met up with him when he was alone in the wilderness—and almost all of them carried guns.

"Do you know anything about all those women who died?"

Henry's question startled him, but he told himself it shouldn't have surprised him. The Ice Cold Killer was the number one topic of conversation in Eagle Mountain these days. Henry had probably heard his customers and his family talking about the case.

"I'm trying to help find the man who killed those women," Nate said.

"Michaela was my friend." Henry's mouth turned down, and his lip quivered. He sniffed. "She worked at the bank and she helped me with my account."

"I'm very sorry you lost your friend," Nate said.

"I saw her the day before she died. She came in here to the store. She did that sometimes. She would buy a salad or fruit for her lunch and say hello to me."

"That's good that you got to see her."

Henry was frowning or maybe concentrating very hard. Nate couldn't tell. "She was with a man," Henry said. "They were laughing and she was smiling at him—different from the way she smiled at me."

The hair on the back of Nate's neck stood up. "Who was the man, do you know?"

Henry shook his head. "I didn't know him. But I think maybe he was her boyfriend."

Nate set the bag of apples in his cart and moved closer to Henry, the way he might approach a skittish deer. "Henry, do you think you would recognize that man if you saw him again?"

He nodded. "I think so. I'm pretty good at remembering people."

"Could you come to the sheriff's department with me and tell them what you told me, and maybe describe the man to them?"

Henry's frown deepened. "I can't come now. I have to work." His voice rose. A couple of shoppers turned to stare.

"What time do you get off work?" Nate asked.

Henry tilted his head to one side, thinking. "I get off today at three o'clock," he said.

"If I come back here at three, will you go to the sheriff's office with me?" Nate asked. "Just for a little bit?"

Henry shrugged. "I guess so. Is it important?"

"Yes. It's important."

"Okay." He turned back to arranging the apples. "See you at three."

Nate finished his shopping, his mind racing. If Henry was telling the truth—and he would have no reason to lie—then he might have seen Michaela with her killer. This might be the break they had been waiting for.

Chapter Eight

Jamie didn't make it back to the grocery store until three fifteen. Donna got off at three, so Jamie reasoned this would be a good opportunity for her to meet Henry without upsetting her sister if things didn't go well. "I'm looking for someone named Henry, who works in your produce department," she told the young woman at the office, whose name tag identified her as Veronique.

"Henry?" Veronique's eyebrows rose. "He's not in any kind of trouble, is he?"

"No, no. I just wanted to meet him. He's, uh, he's friends with my sister, Donna."

"Oh, Donna! Of course." Veronique brightened. "She and Henry left at three. He said something about walking her home." She giggled. "They're so cute together."

So much for Jamie's plan to meet Henry alone. "What is Henry like?" she asked.

"Oh, he's a good kid. Like Donna. He came to us from the same program."

"You mean, he's developmentally disabled, too."

"Yeah. Down syndrome, I think. But a good worker. Friendly. Customers like him. They like Donna, too."

"How old is he?"

"Early twenties. He lives with his mother, I think. Why do you want to know?"

"Donna says he's her boyfriend."

Veronique giggled again. "Yeah, those two are really sweet on each other. It's cute."

"Thanks." Jamie left the store and returned to her cruiser. Henry didn't sound like a serial killer who was going to lure her sister to a remote location and kill her. But she still wanted to meet him. She checked her watch. They might already be at Mrs. Simmons's, but since they were on foot, and Donna was never one to hurry, Jamie ought to be able to catch up with them en route and introduce herself.

She cruised slowly through the streets of Eagle Mountain, waving to people she passed and keeping an eye out for her sister and the mysterious Henry. She pulled into Mrs. Simmons's driveway, wondering if her sister had arrived ahead of her. She hoped Henry hadn't already left. Knowing Mrs. Simmons, she would have invited him in.

The sitter met Jamie on the front porch. "I was getting ready to call you," she said, before Jamie could speak. "Donna isn't here. It's not like her to be so late.'

Jamie tried to push back the fear that climbed in her throat and the painful drumming of her heart. "She left the store at three," she said. "And I didn't see her on the drive over. Maybe I misunderstood where she was going." She squeezed Mrs. Simmons's clasped hands. "I'll go back to the store and talk to them again. Call me right away if she shows up."

Mrs. Simmons nodded, her face creased with worry.

Before heading to the store, Jamie stopped at her house. Donna was always going on about wanting to stay by herself. Maybe when she said she was going home, she meant exactly that, and she had brought Henry here to the house.

But the house was locked up tight, and only the dogs responded to Jamie's calls.

Back at the store, Jamie had to hunt up Veronique in the bakery, where she was accepting an order from a vendor. "Are you sure Donna and Henry said they were headed home?" she asked.

"Yes." Veronique looked up from her clipboard. "I spoke to him myself when he was punching out."

"Maybe he meant his home. Can you give me his parents' number?"

Veronique's brow furrowed. "We're not supposed to give out personal information about our employees."

"I'm a sheriff's deputy. And I'm trying to make sure my sister is safe." Jamie couldn't rein in her impatience.

"Oh, uh, okay."

Jamie followed the woman to the front office, and a few moments later was dialing the number for Mrs. O'Keefe. While she listened to the phone ring, she thought about the approach she should take with these people. She didn't want to send them into a panic.

"Hello?" a woman answered.

"Hello, Mrs. O'Keefe?"

"Yes."

"This is Jamie Douglas. I'm Donna Douglas's sister. She works with your son, Henry, at the grocery store."

"Oh, yes," the woman's voice softened. "We've met Donna before." She chuckled. "Henry is quite taken with her.'

"Have you seen Henry, or talked to him, since he got off work at three?"

"No. He mentioned this morning that he was going to walk Donna to the house where she stays every afternoon while you work. It's only a few blocks, and we do like to encourage Henry to be as independent as possible. He's really very responsible."

Jamie took a deep breath. She hated worrying this woman, who sounded very nice. But in Mrs. O'Keefe's position, she would want to know. "Donna and Henry never showed up at the sitter's," she said. "I'm trying to find them now."

"Oh, no! That doesn't sound like Henry at all." Her voice broke. "You don't think this horrible killer has decided to go after them, do you?"

"I'm sure that's not it," Jamie said, as much to reassure herself as to allay Mrs. O'Keefe's fears. "They probably decided to stop off at a restaurant or something. Donna mentioned this morning that she and Henry wanted to go on a date."

"Yes. Yes, that sounds reasonable." Mrs. O'Keefe was clearly trying to keep it together.

"I'm a sheriff's deputy," Jamie said. "We'll start looking for them right away. I'll call you as soon as I know anything."

"Please do. This is so unlike Henry. He's such a good boy. Well, he's a man now, of course, but he'll always be my boy."

"I understand." Jamie sometimes had to remind herself that, while Donna would always be her little sister, she was a grown woman.

"Is everything all right?" Veronique asked when Jamie ended the call.

"I'm sure they're fine," Jamie said. "I'm going to look for them."

She checked the most likely spots first—the Cakewalk Café, Peggy's Pizza and Kate's—but no one had seen Donna or Henry, together or alone. As Jamie cruised down Eagle Mountain's main drag, she scanned the sidewalks and shops for any sign of the two young people.

Tense with worry, she headed for the sheriff's department. She hated to involve the department in her family's business, but she needed her fellow officers' help in tracking down Donna and Henry before they got into trouble. Anyone could take advantage of two such trusting souls.

She parked on the street and entered through the front door. If Travis wasn't in his office, Adelaide would know where to find him.

But when Jamie approached Adelaide's desk, she

discovered the office manager wasn't alone. "Hey, Jamie!" Donna stood and hurried around Adelaide's desk to hug her sister.

Jamie hugged her back and had to wait a few seconds before she felt safe speaking. "What are you doing here?" she asked Donna.

"I'm waiting for Henry," Donna said, as if this explained everything.

"Donna's friend is giving a statement to the sheriff," Adelaide said.

"A statement about what?"

"I don't know," Adelaide said. "Nate brought him in."

"Nate Hall?" How was Nate involved in any of this?

"He gave us a ride in his truck," Donna said. "He has a set of deer antlers and a shotgun in it."

"I don't understand," Jamie said. "Did something happen?" She addressed her sister. "Did someone try to hurt you and Henry while you were walking home?"

Donna looked puzzled. "No. We came here with Nate, in his truck."

"I'm sure he'll be finished in a few minutes," Adelaide said. "Then you can ask the sheriff what this is about."

Not knowing what else to do, Jamie sat, only half paying attention to the conversation Donna and Adelaide were having about the masquerade ball on Friday. After about five minutes, the door to the sheriff's office opened and Nate emerged with a stocky young man who wore black framed glasses. The young man—Henry—grinned as Donna rushed to meet him. "I still need to walk you home," he said.

"Hello, Henry. I'm Donna's sister, Jamie." Jamie offered her hand and Henry solemnly shook it.

"Nice to meet you," he said.

Jamie looked past him to address Nate, who supported himself with crutches. "What are Henry and my sister doing here at the sheriff's department?"

"Henry was friends with Michaela Underwood," Nate said. "He saw her in the store the day before she died, with a man he thought was her boyfriend."

"Al," Jamie said. The man who might have been her killer.

"He gave us a very good description of the man," Nate said. "He's been a big help to us."

"I need to walk Donna home now," Henry said.

"I'll drive Donna home," Jamie said. "And I need to call your mother, Henry. When you didn't come home, she was worried. The way Mrs. Simmons and I were worried about Donna when she didn't show up on time." She glared at Nate as she said the last words. He had the grace to look chagrined.

"I'll give you a ride to your place, Henry," Nate said. "After we call your mom."

Jamie already had her phone out and was dialing the O'Keefes' number. Mrs. O'Keefe answered after the first ring. "Henry is fine," Jamie said. "He and Donna are here at the sheriff's department. Everything is all right. They're not in trouble. Henry was able to give some evidence in a case we're working on. An officer is going to bring him home... Of course, if you would rather. I understand." She chatted with Mrs. O'Keefe for another minute and then ended the call. "Your mother is coming to get you," she told Henry.

"I'll wait with him, if you want to go," Nate said.

"No, I do not want to go." Jamie took Nate's arm and tugged him toward the hallway. Reluctantly, he hobbled after her.

She led the way into the empty conference room and shut the door behind him. He held up his hand to stop her speaking. "Before you lay into me, I realize I screwed up," he said. "I should have let you know what was going on and that your sister was safe. I didn't mean to worry you."

"You didn't mean to worry me? There is a killer out there who preys on women. My sister would be an easy target. I wasn't worried—I was petrified."

"I get that, and I'm sorry." He took her hand, his thumb tracing the contours of her knuckles, the touch reassuring—and unsettling. "I'm really sorry. I promise not to do that to you again."

She wanted to continue to rage at him but feared that if she opened her mouth again, she'd start crying. She forced back the tears and pulled her hand away from his. "How did you find out Henry knew Michaela?" she asked.

"I was buying groceries and we got to talking. He saw my uniform and asked if I knew about the murders—then he told me he had seen Michaela the day before she died, with a man he hadn't seen her with before."

"Then how did my sister get involved?"

"When I showed up at three to pick up Henry and bring him here to make his statement, Donna was with him. He said she needed to come with him and I didn't see any harm in it." He grimaced. "I should have realized you'd be worried."

"I know. And really, Donna should have called me herself. She knows she's supposed to."

"Am I forgiven?" he asked.

His contrite tone almost made her laugh. The tension of the afternoon had her emotions ricocheting all over the place. "I'll think about it," she said, moving past him.

Henry and Donna waited where Nate and Jamie had left them, seated in chairs by the door, holding hands. "I want to take Donna to the party Friday night," Henry said, standing as Nate and Jamie approached.

"We're supposed to wear costumes," Donna said, bouncing on her toes with excitement.

Jamie opened her mouth to say no. Donna needed to stay home, where she would be safe. But she couldn't keep her sister a prisoner. And Jamie had planned to attend the masquerade party anyway. "All right," she said.

Donna looked to Henry, who nodded. "Good," he said.

Jamie took her sister's hand. "Come on. I'll take you to Mrs. Simmons's," she said.

"See you tomorrow," Henry said. He stopped and blew Donna a kiss. She returned the gesture, blushing and giggling. Jamie couldn't help smiling. Veronique was right—Donna and Henry made a cute couple. She was happy Donna had found a friend, but her heart ached at the knowledge that no matter how hard she tried, she could never protect her sister from all the ways the world could hurt her.

NATE HAD JUST settled onto the sofa, feet up, a cup of cocoa in one hand, a suspense novel in the other, when someone rapped on his door. "Who is it?" he called. He could count on the fingers of one hand the number of people who had stopped by for a visit since he had moved in four months ago.

"It's Travis."

Intrigued, Nate levered himself to his feet and clomped to the door with the aid of one crutch. He unlocked it and opened it to admit the sheriff. "I wanted to see how you're doing and check if you needed anything," Travis said.

"Thanks, but I'm okay." Nate dropped back onto the sofa. He doubted the sheriff had really come over to check on him. Travis had something on his mind. Even back in college, when they had roomed together, Travis had a tendency to brood. "Have a seat," Nate said.

Travis sat, elbows on his knees, hands clasped in front of his mouth, saying nothing.

"How are the wedding preparations going?" Nate asked. "It won't be long now."

"They're going okay. Lacy is a little anxious about the weather. Some of the guests won't be able to attend if the road doesn't open."

"You won't be able to get away for your honeymoon, either," Nate said.

"I'm not going anywhere until this killer is caught. Lacy knows that."

"You never were one to leave a job unfinished. What's the latest?"

"We can't get a police artist to come here, because of the road closures, but I've arranged for one to Skype with Henry O'Keefe. I'm hoping we can get an image we can publish in the paper and distribute around town. Someone knows this guy."

"He may not be the killer."

"Maybe not. But he might have seen something that morning that could help us find the killer." He sat up straight. "He's going to strike again, I'm sure."

"What about the plan to have Jamie drive around, trying to attract the killer's attention?" Nate didn't like the idea, but it wasn't his decision to make.

"We're going to do that tonight," Travis said. "I put it off one night after we got the description from Henry. I wanted to see if that led to anyone obvious. It didn't, but maybe we'll have better luck with the drawing. Meanwhile, Dwight is going out with Jamie tonight. Gage and I will be on duty nearby, ready to close in."

"Jamie is pretty new to the force, isn't she?"

"She's been with us almost a year. She's been a good addition to the department."

"I knew her growing up," Nate said. "I never would have dreamed she'd go into law enforcement. It's not anything she ever talked about." Whereas he had decided to aim for a job with Parks and Wildlife when he was still in his teens. The idea of being able to study wildlife and actively protect it, while also helping to educate the public, had appealed to him, as had the freedom to spend lots of time outdoors.

"She's hardworking and good with people," Travis said. "She's smart. And we're working to diversify the force to better reflect the population we serve. We're hoping to recruit more women like her."

"She seems to really like the work. But are you sure she's up for this decoy exercise tonight? This killer—or killers—has made a habit of killing women very quickly." His stomach clenched as he spoke.

Travis's gaze met Nate's, unwavering. "I wouldn't ask Jamie to do this if I didn't believe she could handle it," he said. "So, what's going on between you two?"

Nate looked away. "Nothing is going on between us."

"I thought I sensed some…tension."

Nate laughed. "Oh, there's tension all right. She can't stand me."

"And why is that?"

He blew out a breath. Travis wasn't the type to press if Nate told him to mind his own business, but maybe getting his levelheaded friend's perspective would help. "Jamie and I dated during high school," he said. "We were really close. I guess you could say we were each other's first love. But then it was time to go to college and I was going away. I didn't think it was fair to ask her to wait for me, so I broke things off with her. I thought we could still be friends, but she didn't see it that way." His shoulders sagged. "I guess you could say things ended badly. Apparently, she's never forgiven me. Maybe because I wasn't around to support her after her parents died."

"It takes a lot of energy to hold on to anger that long," Travis said. "It makes me think there's more than animosity behind it."

"Think that if you like, but she's made it clear she doesn't want to have anything to do with me."

Travis's phone rang and he answered. He listened for a moment, frowning, then stood. "I'm on my way." He pocketed his phone again. "That was Adelaide," he said. "The Ice Cold Killer has struck again—only this time, the woman got away."

Chapter Nine

"You're going to be all right, Tammy. You're safe now." Jamie handed the distraught young woman a cup of water, then sat next to her, pulling the chair close. Tammy Patterson, reporter for the *Eagle Mountain Examiner*, had stumbled into the sheriff's department ten minutes before, her clothes torn, her face bloodied, tears running down her cheeks. She had sobbed incoherently, something about the Ice Cold Killer coming after her. "You're safe now," Jamie murmured again and pressed a cold compress to the swelling on the side of Tammy's face.

"The sheriff is on his way," Dwight Prentice said from the doorway of the conference room. "The paramedics are coming, too."

Jamie nodded. It wouldn't hurt to have Tammy's bruises checked. "Drink some water," she urged. "When the sheriff gets here, we'll need you to tell us what happened, but remember, you're safe and you're with friends."

Tammy nodded and drank. Her hands didn't shake as badly now, and the flow of tears had subsided.

Dwight glanced over this shoulder. "Sheriff's here." A moment later, Travis entered.

"Hello, Tammy," he said. "I understand you've had a frightening time of it."

She drew in a deep, shuddering breath. "I was terrified. But I'm alive and safe now—that's what counts."

Travis pulled up a chair across from Tammy. "You may be able to help us catch this guy and stop him from hurting other women. So I need you to tell me everything you can remember about what happened—even if the detail seems too small to be important. Can you do that?"

She nodded, licked her lips and began speaking, hesitantly at first, then with more assurance. "I was out on County Road Two. Colorado Parks and Wildlife is going to start putting out food for the deer and elk who have been stressed by all this snow, and they have a staging area out there for the supplies and volunteers. I went out there to get photos for the paper."

She took a sip of water, then continued. "I was on my way back to town, maybe three miles from the staging area. It had started snowing, and visibility wasn't that good. Then all of a sudden, I saw a woman standing on the side of the road. She was waving her arms. I had to stop. I pulled over to the shoulder and she ran up to the passenger side of the car. I rolled down the window and she told me she had had a fight with her boyfriend, who was drunk. She needed to get to town—or at least to borrow a phone so she could call a friend to come get her. Of course I said

I'd help her. She was so distressed—clearly, she had been crying, and her hair was all down in her eyes, and she sounded almost hysterical. I unlocked the car and leaned over to clear stuff off the passenger seat so she could get in."

She closed her eyes and a shudder went through her. "All of a sudden, the driver's-side door opened and someone grabbed me and started hauling me out of the car. I screamed and started trying to fight him off. I thought at first it was the woman's boyfriend, angry because I was getting involved. But then the woman came around to the side of the road. While he held my arms, she grabbed at my legs and started trying to wrap them with duct tape."

"The woman was helping him?" Jamie asked.

Tammy's eyes met hers. "Looking back now, I don't think it really was a woman," she said. "This person was really strong."

"Do you think it was a man, dressed up like a woman?" Travis asked.

"Maybe," Tammy said. "She was tall for a woman, and she had lots of blond hair, all falling in front of her face. She never really looked directly at me. I think the hair might have been a wig. And like I said, she was so strong."

Travis nodded. "All right. Tell us about the other man. The one who grabbed you."

Tammy shook her head. "There's not much to tell. He was behind me most of the time. I only saw him for a few seconds, from the side. He was dressed all in black, with a ski mask pulled down over his head."

"How tall do you think he was?" Travis asked. "How much taller than you?"

"He was taller than me—most men are. But he wasn't really tall, so I'd say, maybe five-ten. But the ground was really uneven there, and he was behind me, so he might have been six feet tall, just standing on lower ground."

"What about build?" Travis asked. "Was he stocky, or really muscular?"

She shook her head. "No, he was just, you know, average. I wish now I had paid more attention, but I was so scared. I was sure he was going to kill me."

"You got away," Jamie reminded her. "You're safe."

"What did you do?" Travis asked. "How did you get away?"

"I fought so hard. When he grabbed me, I had picked up my notebook off the passenger seat so the woman could get in. It had a pen clipped to it. I grabbed the pen and stabbed at him—at his hands, his face. And I kicked at the woman. She dropped the duct tape and it rolled into the dirt." Tammy's eyes widened. "I remember now—she swore, and her voice was different—deeper. A man's voice."

"Did he say a name, or address the other man in any way?" Travis asked.

Tammy closed her eyes. Jamie imagined her putting herself back in that place. "No. They didn't say anything to each other. The man in the ski mask was angry that I fought, and he hit me—hard." She put a hand to her bruised face. "But I was so terrified. I knew if I didn't get away from them, I would die.

So I did everything I could think of. I kept stabbing with the pen, and I spat at him and tried to bite him. When he dragged me from the car, I hooked one foot onto the bottom of the seat. It threw him off balance. The side of the road is really rough over there, and there's a lot of snow. He slid down into the ditch, away from me. I got up and crawled back into the car and slammed the door. The engine was still running, so I just floored it. I almost ran over the woman.

"I don't even remember getting here. I just drove, as fast as I could. I kept looking in the mirror, to see if they followed me, but they didn't."

"Where were you, exactly, when this happened?" Travis asked.

"On County Road Two. There's that little neighborhood of houses in there, then a stretch of woods, then a big curve. This was right after the big curve."

"You want me to go out and take a look?" Dwight spoke from the doorway.

"Take Gage with you. Find the scene and cordon it off. Do a search, then hit the houses around there. Talk to everyone you can. Find out if they know anything. Or saw or heard anything"

"That's only a few miles from where Michaela's body was found," Jamie said. "The killers might live in one of those houses."

"I want to go out there tonight, see if we can draw them out." Travis said. He turned to Jamie. "If you're still up for it, Deputy."

"I am."

"I'll call Gage," Dwight said, and left them as two

paramedics entered. Travis and Jamie moved away to let them check out Tammy.

"You don't have to do this decoy op if you're uncomfortable with it," Travis told Jamie. "There's no doubt these two are dangerous."

"I want to, sir," she said. "This may be our best chance to catch them. They'll be frustrated that Tammy got away."

"I agree." He clapped her on the shoulder. "Go home now and change."

"Yes, sir." She glanced at Tammy. "What about her?"

"She lives with her parents here in town. I'll call them in a minute and they can come pick her up. She should be safe there, but I'll put a reserve deputy on the house tonight, just in case. Be back here at seven o'clock."

"Yes, sir." She hurried from the room, buzzing with excitement. She might be able to catch these killers—tonight.

"You're being an idiot," Nate mumbled to himself as he grabbed his crutches and swung out of the cab of his truck. He had just pulled into Jamie's driveway. It was six thirty at night. Her car was in the driveway, and most of the windows of the house were lit up, so he was pretty sure she was home. She'd probably be furious to see him. He should leave her alone. But, knowing she was going out there tonight, possibly to face a serial killer—or more than one serial killer— he couldn't stay away.

He positioned the crutches under his arms and paused a moment to look up at the house. The place didn't look that much different than it had when he was in high school, at least in the dark. The same stone lions sat on either side of the steps leading up to the wide front porch, and the same wooden swing hung from the porch rafters. He and Jamie had spent many hours on that swing, sometimes making out, but mostly talking, about everything. He hadn't been able to talk to anyone like that since. Maybe it was only as a teenager that a man could be comfortable baring his soul that way. Or maybe he could only do it with Jamie.

He clumped his way up the walk, navigated the steps, crossed the porch and rang the doorbell. It echoed loudly through the house. "I'll get it!" a voice shouted, followed by the thunder of running feet on a hardwood floor.

The door opened and Donna peeked out. "Hello," she said, then held the door open wider. "Come in."

Jamie appeared behind her sister. She caught the door and held it. "What are you doing here?" she asked.

"I just wanted to talk, okay? Please?"

Reluctantly, she let him in. "I don't have much time," she said as he moved past her. "I have to be at the sheriff's department at seven."

"I know what you're going to do tonight," he said.

"I'm going to do my job."

"You're sure dressed up for work," Donna said.

Nate let his gaze slide over the short blue dress,

with its low-cut neckline and full, swirly skirt. It was made of some soft fabric that hugged her curves, and the skirt stopped several inches above the tops of the tall black boots she wore. A sudden pull of attraction caught him off guard.

"Donna, I left my purse upstairs," Jamie said. "Could you get it for me, please?"

When Donna had left them, Jamie turned back to Nate. "Why are you staring at me that way?"

"Is that what you're wearing tonight?" he asked.

"Yes."

"You'll have on a coat, right?"

"My car has a heater. I don't want these two to have any doubt that I'm a young woman."

Yeah, there was no doubt of that. "You should wear a vest," he said.

Her eyebrows rose. "You mean a tactical vest?"

"Yes."

"These two use a knife," she said. "They don't shoot people. And they slit throats. A tactical vest wouldn't be any help at all."

"You don't know they don't have a gun."

"They didn't use it on Tammy today. If they had one, you'd think they would have."

"Tammy? Is that the woman who got away from the killer? Travis got the call while he was at my house."

"Killers. There are two of them."

"What happened this afternoon?" he asked. "You can tell me—I'm part of the team and I'm going to hear about it in the briefing tomorrow morning any-way."

She crossed her arms over her chest. She probably didn't realize how much it enhanced her cleavage. Nate shifted, hoping she didn't notice the effect she was having on him. "Aren't you on medical leave?" she asked.

"From my Parks and Wildlife job—not from the team that's hunting this killer. I can sort data and do research with one foot in a cast. So what happened to Tammy? And Tammy who?"

Jamie glanced up the stairs, then lowered her voice. "Tammy Patterson—the reporter for the paper? She stopped to help a woman who flagged her down. Only it wasn't a woman—it was a man in a wig. A second man came out of the woods and grabbed Tammy and he and the one dressed like a woman tried to wrap her up in duct tape. Tammy fought like a wildcat and managed to get away."

"She was lucky."

"Yes. And she may be our lucky break. I'm really hoping we catch these two tonight." She took a step back. "You still haven't told me why you're here."

"I just—" He shoved his hands in his pockets. He'd feel better if he could pace, but that was impossible on crutches. "I just wanted to tell you to be careful." He couldn't believe how lame he sounded, but he hadn't thought this out very well—he had just gotten in his truck and started to drive, and ended up here.

"I'm not an idiot," she said.

"I know that. But neither are these killers."

"Why do you care, anyway?" she asked.

"Because I do." Their eyes met and the heat in her gaze rocked him back. Jamie might *say* she couldn't stand him, but that was not what it felt like right now. He leaned toward her. Another half second and he would have to kiss her. She looked like she wanted to kiss him back. He just needed to be a little closer…

"Here's your purse. It wasn't upstairs, it was on the kitchen table." Donna came into the room, the purse dangling from her wrist. Jamie looked away and Nate suppressed a groan of disappointment. "Are you going to stay with me while Jamie goes out?" Donna asked.

"Nate isn't going to stay with you," Jamie said. "You're going to Mrs. Simmons's."

"I could stay with her," Nate said. "I don't mind." And he'd be here when Jamie got home, to make sure she was all right.

"Yay!" Donna clapped her hands. "Do you like to play cards? We can play cards."

"Donna, I don't think—" Jamie began.

"Really, I don't mind," Nate said. "Let me stay."

"Pleeeease!" Donna put her hands together as if praying. "I don't want to go to Mrs. Simmons's all the time. I want to stay here."

Jamie blew out a breath. "Okay." She frowned at Nate. "I guess I will feel better, knowing she's with you."

"She'll be safe with me," Nate said. If he couldn't look after Jamie, at least he could look after her sister. "THIS FEELS REALLY WEIRD," Jamie said, as she drove slowly along County Road Two, constantly scanning the side of the road for any sign of life. The afternoon's snow had stopped, and the plows had left fresh drifts on the roadside that reflected back the glow from her headlights.

"Imagine how I feel." Dwight Prentice spoke from his position on the floorboard of the back seat.

Jamie grimaced, remembering the awkward contortions required for the six-foot-three deputy to hide in her car. "We're passing that neighborhood Tammy mentioned," she said.

"The place where she pulled over is around the next big curve," Dwight said. "By the time we got there, the new snow had almost covered the area. By now the plows will have wiped out everything—not that there was anything to find. We didn't see so much as a hair or a button."

Jamie cruised slowly past the spot, where yellow crime scene tape fluttered from roadside brush. "We haven't even passed another car in ten minutes," she said.

"When you can find a place to turn around, go ahead and do so," Dwight said. "We'll make one more pass past that neighborhood. Pretend you're looking for an address. If you don't attract any attention after that, we'll call it a night."

"Maybe Tammy getting away scared them off," Jamie said, as she pulled over onto the shoulder and prepared to turn around.

"They can't have gone far," Dwight said. "The highway out of town is still closed."

She swung the car around, then gasped and slammed on the brakes as her headlights lit up the figure of a man on the side of the road. He put up one hand to shield his eyes, then hunched over and turned back toward the woods. Jamie shoved open the door and bailed out of the car, her Glock already drawn. "Stop, police!"

Jamie heard Dwight move in behind her. The man, who wore a fur cap with earflaps and sported a full beard, dropped two items and raised his hands over his head. "Don't shoot," he pleaded.

"Get on your knees," Dwight ordered. "Hands behind your head."

The man did as asked and Dwight moved in closer, Jamie behind him. She nudged at the rifle the man had dropped and what she now recognized as a handheld spotlight. The first rush of adrenaline was fading, leaving behind a sinking feeling. "Who are you, and what are you doing out here in the middle of the night?" he asked.

"It's only nine o'clock," he said.

"What's your name?" she asked.

The man—who up close looked to be at least seventy—looked away and didn't answer.

Dwight rummaged in the man's pocket and pulled out a wallet. He flipped it open and read. "Mitch Oliphant." He looked at the man. "What were you doing out here, Mr. Oliphant?"

Again, no answer.

Jamie nudged the spotlight with her toe. "It looks to me like you were spotlighting deer," she said. "Which is against the law."

"You ain't no game warden," Oliphant said.

No. The local game warden was currently at Jamie's house, babysitting her sister.

"In fact, how do I know you're even a cop?" Oliphant continued. "You sure ain't dressed like one." He leered and she suppressed the urge to tug on her short skirt.

"We can still enforce the law," she said. "How long have you been out here tonight?"

"There's no law against being out at night. I was taking a walk."

"With your rifle and a spotlight?" Dwight asked.

"I couldn't find my flashlight. And a man's got a right to defend himself, with that crazy killer running around."

"What do you know about the killer?" Jamie asked.

Oliphant glared at her. "Nothing."

"Have you seen anyone else while you were taking your walk?" Jamie asked. "Anyone at all?"

"No. Can I get up now? Being down on the ground like this hurts my knees."

Jamie and Dwight exchanged glances. "You can get up," Jamie said. "Slowly."

"At my age, that's the only speed I got." Grunting, Oliphant rose to his feet. "Are you gonna keep me standing out here in the cold all night?" he asked.

"Where do you live?" Dwight asked.

"The address is on my license." Oliphant stared at Dwight, who didn't back down. Jamie focused on the two, trying to ignore her freezing feet and wishing she had thought to get her coat from the car. "I live out on Fish Camp Road," Oliphant finally said.

Jamie gaped. That had to be at least eight miles from where they were standing. "Did you walk all the way from there?"

"No. My truck is parked up the road about a quarter mile." He jerked his head toward town.

"We'll let you go if you promise to go home and stay there," Dwight said. "Don't be out here at night where you don't have any business."

Oliphant muttered something to the effect that it was a free country and turned away, but Jamie called after him. "Mr. Oliphant?"

He glanced back at her. "What?"

"Do you come out here often? Walking?"

"What's it to you?"

"You might be able to help us. We're looking for a woman—a tall blonde. A couple of people have seen her out here, walking along the road. She told one woman who stopped to help her that she had a boyfriend who beats her. We want to make sure she's all right." It was close enough to the truth.

The lines between Oliphant's brows deepened. "I think I saw her, once. But when she saw me, she took off—right into the woods, like a scared rabbit."

"Did you get a good look at her?" Dwight asked. "Do you think you'd recognize her again?"

The old man shook his head. "I only saw her for a few seconds. She was tall and thin, with a lot of blond hair, all hanging down in her face."

"Where were you when you saw her?" Jamie asked.

He looked around them. "I don't know. Somewhere around here. I can't remember."

"When did you see her?" Dwight asked.

"A week ago? Maybe more." He shrugged. "It was just a few seconds. I didn't mark it on my calendar or anything."

Jamie glanced at Dwight. He shook his head slightly, indicating he didn't have anything to add. "All right, Mr. Oliphant, you can go," Jamie said. "If we have any more questions, we'll be in touch."

He picked up his rifle and the spotlight, then shuffled away, down the shoulder of the road. Jamie got back into the car and turned the heat up to high. Dwight slid into the passenger seat. "What do you make of his story about the blonde?" he asked, as she turned onto the highway and headed for town.

"It sounds like these two troll for women pretty regularly," she said. "The guy dressed up in the wig is the bait to get the women to stop, then his friend comes out of the woods. Together, they subdue and kill the women." She shuddered. "Creepy."

"Travis is going to get a police artist with Tammy and see if we can get a portrait we can circulate," Dwight said.

"He probably only wears the disguise when they're out hunting," Jamie said.

"Maybe the artist can give us an idea of what the guy looks like without a wig."

"Maybe." She yawned. "I hate that we didn't lure them out tonight."

"You didn't hesitate when we saw Oliphant," Dwight said. "That was good."

"I knew you had my back."

She drove to the sheriff's department, where she and Dwight made their report to the sheriff, then she headed for home. It was all she could do to stay awake for the drive. The tension of the day had drained her. As she pulled into the driveway, she saw that someone had left the porch light on for her. The door opened while she was still standing on the porch, fumbling for her keys, and she walked in—right into Nate's arms.

Chapter Ten

The strength of Nate's embrace felt so familiar—so right. Jamie closed her eyes and rested her head on his shoulder, breathing in the clean, masculine scent of him, feeling as if she could let go completely, and he would continue to hold her up. "Tough night?" he asked after a moment, his voice low, his warm breath stirring her hair.

She lifted her head and looked up at him. "We didn't see the killers," she said. "We stopped and questioned an old man. I think he was spotlighting deer, but we couldn't prove it, so we had to let him go."

"Who was it?" Nate asked.

"Mitch Oliphant."

He nodded. "I know Mitch. And yeah, he was probably spotlighting deer." He frowned. "Did he do something to upset you?"

"No. I'm just tired. Seeing Tammy this afternoon and then going out there tonight—it's a lot to take in."

"You've had to be strong for a long time." He smoothed his hand down her arm. "You've carried a lot of weight on your shoulders for the past few years. I'm sorry I wasn't there for you then. But I'm here for you now."

His words—and the meaning behind them—were more seductive than any sexy love-words. She prided herself on standing on her own two feet, but some-times—times like tonight—it was so hard. To be able to lean on someone else, just for a little while, was a luxury she craved the way some people wanted sex or money. She stared into his eyes, trying to figure out the catch to his words—to figure out what he expected from her in exchange for his help. But she saw nothing but tenderness, and allowed herself to let down her guard just a little.

Just long enough for one kiss. She closed her eyes as his lips met hers, letting her body soften and mold to his. They kissed as if they had been apart only a few hours instead of seven years. She tilted her head to deepen the kiss and he tasted both familiar and new. She had missed this—this closeness, this com-municating without words, this swell of desire and need and the promise of fulfillment. She had been here before with him, and yet she wasn't kissing a boy this time but a man, with a man's power and knowl-edge and patience. The thought thrilled her and had her wondering if they could sneak upstairs to her bedroom without Donna hearing them.

She eased back slightly and opened her eyes. He was smiling—a look filled with triumph. That gleam of victory set her back on her heels. She shoved away from him and raked a hand through her hair, trying to think. "Hey." He reached for her. "It's okay."

"No, it is not okay," she said. Her heart hammered and her buzzing nerves left her feeling shaky and off-balance. "This is a mistake. A big mistake."

"You've got to give me something to do." The next morning, Nate leaned on one crutch in front of the sheriff's desk and pleaded with Travis. "I'm going nuts sitting at the house staring at the walls." With nothing else to occupy his mind, he kept replaying that kiss with Jamie. He'd finally broken through the wall she had erected between them, and she'd let him know she still cared for him—and the next thing he knew, she'd been shoving him out the door, muttering that she "couldn't do this," deaf to his pleas for an explanation.

Travis shifted his gaze to the dark blue Aircast that encased Nate's left ankle. "How long are you off duty?" he asked.

"Until the doctor clears me to return. He says that could be as long as six weeks, but I'm going to be back before then."

Sure you are. Travis had the grace not to say the words out loud, but Nate could read his friend well enough. "Look," he said. "My ankle is busted, not my brain. Haven't you got data that needs crunching, or investigation notes that need reviewing? You need help, don't you?"

"Yes." Travis shoved back his chair and stood. He motioned for Nate to follow him and led the way to a room that was apparently dedicated to the investigation. Photographs of the victims and their crime scenes filled the walls, two long tables contained tagged evidence, and another table held a computer terminal and stacks of paperwork.

Jamie looked up from her seat at this table. Her face paled, then reddened as she stared at Nate. With her cheeks flushed and several tendrils of hair escaping from the knot at the base of her neck, she struck Nate as incredibly desirable—a thought he immediately shoved to the back of his mind. "Nate's going to help you with that witness database," Travis said, then left them.

The sound of the door closing behind Travis echoed in the still room. The plastic chair Nate grabbed from a row against the wall protested loudly as he dragged it to the table. He sat opposite Jamie, who focused on the computer screen. He waited, deciding he'd let her speak first.

"I'm compiling a database of every witness we've interviewed so far," she said after a long, uncomfortable moment. "We need to review their statements, look for similarities, or anything that stands out, and decide if we want to interview them again. You can start reading over their statements while I input the data." She nodded to the stack of file folders at her elbow.

"All right." He took a couple of inches of folders off the top of the pile and placed them in front of him but didn't open one, his eyes steady on her.

After another long moment, she looked over at him. "What?" she asked.

"We need to clear the air between us," he said.

She looked back at the computer, though her hands remained motionless on the keyboard. "I don't know what you're talking about."

"Yes, you do. Ever since I came back to town, you've been giving me the cold shoulder."

She started to shake her head, but he continued. He hadn't really planned to say all this, but now that he was talking, it felt good to get his feelings out in the open. "I get that you were hurt when I broke things off when I went to college," he said. "I'm sorry about that. I really am. But that was seven years ago. We're both adults now. I can't believe you're still holding a stupid thing I did back then over my head."

"I'm not!" She put both hands to her head, as if she wanted to yank out her hair, then lowered them to the table, fists clenched. Her eyes met his and he saw again the pain there, and felt the corresponding ache in his own chest. "You think because we were…involved before, we can be again," she said. "And that's not going to happen."

"You say that—but when you kissed me last night, I wasn't getting that message at all."

Now she looked as if she wanted to throw something at him. He prepared to duck. She glanced toward the door, as if to reassure herself they were still alone. She shifted her gaze back to him. "That kiss last night wasn't about any emotional attachment," she said. "You want me to admit I'm attracted to you—all right, I will. I'm sure that makes you very happy. But you were right when you said we're both adults now. I'm mature enough to know that a relationship between the two of us would be a bad idea."

"Why do you say that?" He leaned across the table toward her, his hands inches from hers, though not touching. "I was serious when I said I care about you," he said. "There was a time when you were the best friend I had. You probably know me better than most people. Why would it be so horrible if we got together?"

"It might be wonderful, for a while." She sounded wistful. "But it wouldn't last. There's no point putting myself through all that."

How do you know it won't last? he started to ask, but couldn't get the words out. Because really, she was right. He had dated at least a dozen women since he had moved away. None seriously. And he wasn't looking for serious with her. At least he didn't think so. She really did know him better than anyone else, didn't she?

He slid his hands away and sat back. "Then we don't have to be lovers," he said. "If I agree to respect that boundary, can we at least be friends? Can we work as a team on this case without this—this coldness between us?"

She hesitated, then looked him in the eye. "Yes. We can do that."

He was a little embarrassed at how much he wanted to whoop and celebrate over such a simple thing. He settled for nodding and opened the file folder on the top of his pile. "All right," he said. "Glad we got that settled. Let's get to work."

JAMIE WAS SURPRISED to find she missed Nate after he left at two for a doctor's appointment. After their awkward—but she could admit now, probably necessary—conversation, they had settled into an efficient and, yes, friendly, work pattern. She was reminded of how smart he was—organized and quick to winnow out nonessential information and grasp patterns, traits that probably helped him with wildlife research. She couldn't help but be reminded of all those afternoons they had spent studying together—he coaching her through chemistry and advanced algebra, she helping him with English and history. They each brought different strengths to the table, and it was the same this afternoon. With his help, she was able to get every witness into the database, and had almost completed summarizing what each one had to say by the time she clocked out at six. Tomorrow she'd finish up and begin indexing by keyword, and focus on people they needed to interview again.

Donna also worked until six today, so Jamie swung by the grocery store and picked her up. She was waiting out front with Henry, the two holding hands. Jamie smiled in spite of herself. They really were a cute couple, and they looked so happy. There was something to be said for the naivety of first love—before you knew how much it hurt when things turned sour.

Nate hadn't even tried to deny that he wasn't interested in a long-term romance. At least he'd been honest, and he had confirmed her instinct to avoid falling for him again. They would keep things friendly but platonic.

If Jamie had thought Donna would distract her from thoughts of the handsome wildlife officer, her hope was in vain. "Did you see Nate today?" Donna asked as Jamie drove toward home.

Jamie tightened her hands on the steering wheel. "Why would I see Nate?" she asked.

"You work together, don't you?"

Not exactly. Of course, they had worked together today. "I saw Nate at work today," she said.

"He's cuuuute," Donna said, using one of her favorite descriptions. "I like him. Is he going to come over again soon?"

"I don't think so," Jamie said.

"Why not? You like him, don't you?"

"I like Nate as a friend."

Donna giggled. "I think you like him more than that."

"No. I do not."

"Then why did you kiss him last night? You don't kiss friends like that."

"Donna!" She glanced at her sister. "What were you doing watching us?"

"I heard you come in last night. I wanted to say goodnight. Then I saw you two kissing." She put a hand to her mouth, giggling again. "Is he a good kisser?"

Jamie groaned. She couldn't begin to explain her

complicated feelings for Nate—and how much she regretted that kiss—to her sister. "You shouldn't spy on people," she said. "It isn't nice."

"Henry kissed me."

Jamie blinked and almost missed the turn into their driveway. At the last minute, she braked and steered the car up to the garage. She had talked to Donna about sex more than once over the years, and was confident her sister understood what was and wasn't appropriate behavior. But how much of a defense was that understanding when it came to overheated hormones? Jamie had all but thrown herself at Nate last night in a moment of weakness. She needed to know more about how Donna felt about this new relationship with Henry.

Jamie switched off the car, took a deep breath and turned to her sister. "When did Henry kiss you?" she asked, sounding much calmer than she felt.

"In the break room last Friday. We had our break together, then he leaned over and kissed me on the cheek." She put a hand to her cheek, a dreamy look in her eyes. "He had really soft lips."

Jamie melted a little, from both relief and a rush of tenderness. "That's very sweet," she said. "Henry sounds like a real gentleman."

"He is," Donna said. "He said his mother told him he has to respect me."

Thank you, Mrs. O'Keefe, Jamie silently breathed. She opened her door. "Come on," she said. "Let's make dinner. How does ravioli sound?"

"Ravioli sounds great!" Donna jumped out of the

FREE BOOKS GIVEAWAY

GET TWO FREE BOOKS & TWO FREE GIFTS WORTH OVER $20!

We pay for everything!

YOU pick your books – WE pay for everything.
You get TWO New Books and TWO Mystery Gifts...absolutely FREE

Dear Reader,

I am writing to announce the launch of a huge **FREE BOOK GIVEAWAY**... and to let you know that YOU are entitled to choose TWO fantastic books that WE pay for.

In return, we ask just one favor: Would you please participate in our brief Reader Survey? We'd love to hear from you.

This FREE BOOK GIVEAWAY means that we pay for *everything!* We'll even cover the shipping, and no purchase is necessary, now or later. So please return your survey today. You'll get **Two Free Books** and **Two Mystery Gifts** altogether worth over **$20!**

Sincerely,

Pam Powers

Pam Powers
for Reader Service

Complete the survey below and return it today to receive 2 FREE BOOKS and FREE GIFTS guaranteed!

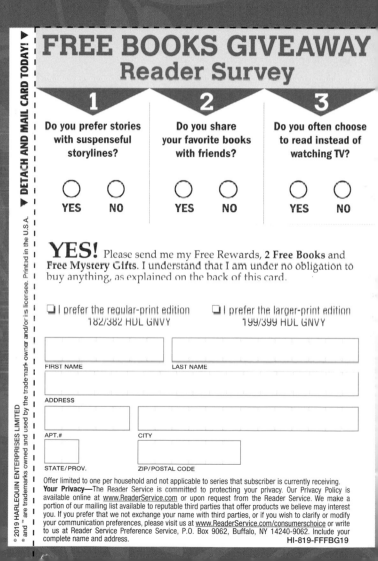

▼ DETACH AND MAIL CARD TODAY! ▼

FREE BOOKS GIVEAWAY
Reader Survey

1

Do you prefer stories with suspenseful storylines?

◯ YES   ◯ NO

2

Do you share your favorite books with friends?

◯ YES   ◯ NO

3

Do you often choose to read instead of watching TV?

◯ YES   ◯ NO

YES! Please send me my Free Rewards, **2 Free Books** and **Free Mystery Gifts**. I understand that I am under no obligation to buy anything, as explained on the back of this card.

❑ I prefer the regular-print edition
182/382 HDL GNVY

❑ I prefer the larger-print edition
199/399 HDL GNVY

FIRST NAME

LAST NAME

ADDRESS

APT.#

CITY

STATE/PROV.

ZIP/POSTAL CODE

HI-819-FFFBG19

car and raced up the walk, all thoughts of Nate and kissing gone.

Together, the sisters made dinner. Donna's job was to set the table and put ice in glasses, a job she did with minimal mess. When she dropped an ice cube, one of the dogs was happy to snatch it up and carry it off to chew. Over supper, Donna told Jamie about helping Mrs. Simmons fold laundry that morning, and a boy she had seen at the store who wore a knit cap made to look like a dinosaur. "I want a hat like that for Christmas," Donna declared.

They were doing dishes when the doorbell rang, sending the dogs into a barking frenzy, toenails scrabbling on the wood floors as they raced to hurl themselves at the intruder. Jamie shouted for them to quiet as she hurried to the front door, then peered out the sidelight at their visitor.

When she opened the door, Tammy Patterson gave her a faint smile. "Hi," she said. "Do you think I could talk to you for a minute?"

"Sure." Jamie's gaze shifted to the street, where a compact car idled, a man at the wheel.

"That's my brother," Tammy said. "He drove me over." She waved at him and he lifted his hand, then put the car in gear and drove away. "He'll pick me up when I call him."

"Come on in." Jamie held open the door. The dogs surged forward to inspect the new arrival, but Jamie shooed them away. Donna watched from the bottom of the stairs. "This is my sister, Donna," Jamie said. "Donna, this is my friend, Tammy."

"Hi, Donna," Tammy said.

"Hi." Donna nibbled her thumb. "Can I watch my show?" she asked.

"Sure. Tammy and I will talk in the kitchen."

Donna hurried off to the living room to insert the cartoon DVD she loved, while Jamie led the way to the kitchen. "Do you want some tea?" she asked, as she filled the kettle.

"Sure." Tammy sat at the table. "I hope you don't mind my coming by," she said. "I had some questions."

"Sure." Jamie put the kettle on, then took the chair opposite Tammy. The bruise on the reporter's cheek had turned a sickly yellow and purple, and there were gray shadows under her eyes. "What can I help you with?" Jamie asked.

"Do you know when I'll get my car back?" Tammy asked.

"I'm not sure. But I can check. You need your car for work, don't you?"

"My mom said I could borrow hers. I just wondered." She ran her thumb back and forth along the edge of the table. "Maybe it's better if I drive my mom's car for a while. The killers wouldn't recognize it."

"You're worried those two are going to come after you, aren't you?" Jamie asked.

Tammy raised her head, her expression bleak. "Shouldn't I be? I'm the only person who's seen them. Well, one of them. If they go ahead and finish the job they started, I won't be able to identify them."

Tammy had a legitimate concern. Under other circumstances, Jamie might have advised the reporter to take a vacation somewhere else until the killers were caught, but that wasn't possible with the roads closed. "I think the best thing you can do right now is to not go anywhere alone," Jamie said. "You were smart to have your brother drive you tonight."

"Yeah, well, that might make it tough to do my job. Of course, I haven't gone back to work yet, though I'll need to soon."

The teakettle whistled and Jamie got up and made the tea. As she poured the water, the smell of apples and cinnamon wafted up on the steam. She hoped the homey smell would help comfort Tammy.

"Do you have any leads in the case?" Tammy asked when Jamie joined her again. "I'm not asking as a reporter."

"You've given us our best lead so far," Jamie said. "But we haven't identified a suspect yet."

"The sheriff has set up a teleconference with a police artist tomorrow," Tammy said. She smoothed her hands down the thighs of her jeans. "I'm really nervous about getting it wrong. I mean, everything happened so fast."

"Police artists are used to working with nervous people," Jamie said. "He—or she—will help you provide the details they need. You probably remember more than you think."

"That's something else that worries me. I know you'll probably think I'm being stupid. I mean, of course I want to find out who is doing this and stop them from killing anyone else. But all along, I've told myself it had to be someone from outside—a stranger to Eagle Mountain who got trapped here by the weather and for whatever reason decided to go on a killing spree."

Jamie nodded. "I think that's a perfectly natural reaction. This seems like such a safe place."

"Right." She bit her lip and looked down at her lap.

"What is it?" Jamie leaned toward the other woman. "Do you know something—have you remembered something—about the killers that might help us catch them?"

Tammy shrugged. "It's nothing, really. Not anything helpful. It's just, well, ever since it happened, I can't shake the feeling that the man in that wig was someone I know. There was something familiar about him. I've tried and tried to think who it could be, but I can't even imagine. But I can't shake the idea that the killer really isn't a stranger. He's someone who lives here. Someone I might even be friends with."

Jamie nodded, an icy knot in the pit of her stomach. "It's always been a possibility—a probability, even. And it would be horrible to find out these two are people we all like, even admire. It's the kind of thing that makes you question your judgment about everyone."

Tammy sighed. "So you don't think I'm crazy?"

"Of course not."

"I promise, I'd tell you if I remembered anything definite," Tammy said.

"You may remember more when you talk to the

artist," Jamie said. She pushed the tea toward Tammy. "Drink up."

Tammy took a long sip of tea, then set the cup down. "I already feel better, talking to you," she said. "Though I don't see how you do the job you do. I mean, I see enough nasty stuff as a reporter, but I only have to take pictures and report. I don't have to wade right into the awful, dangerous stuff or deal with truly horrible people."

"Most of the time the job isn't like that," Jamie said. "The work is interesting, and I believe it's important."

"Good for you." Tammy picked up her cup and smiled at Jamie over its rim. "When this is over, maybe I'll interview you for the paper."

"Why would you want to do that?"

"Eagle Mountain's first female deputy—that's newsworthy, don't you think?"

"Only if we were in the 1950s. I really don't want to call attention to myself."

"I'll keep asking, until you change your mind."

"Right. So what else can we talk about?"

Tammy laughed. "Fair enough. Are you going to the charity masquerade tomorrow night?"

Jamie had already forgotten about the party. "I promised I would. I have to figure out some kind of costume. Will you be there?"

"You bet. I'm even looking forward to it. I mean, if no one else can recognize me in my costume, that means the killers can't, either. I'm hoping I can relax and have a good time."

The two chatted about possible costumes and the weather forecast while they finished their tea, then Tammy phoned her brother. When he arrived, Jamie walked her to the door, but the gist of their conversation kept replaying in her mind. Jamie hadn't thought about the killers being at the party. But if they were locals, why wouldn't they attend and mingle?

And maybe even pick out their next victim.

Chapter Eleven

"Now you remember what I told you?" Jamie adjusted the cat ears atop Donna's head, then looked her sister in the eye. "Tell me."

"I'm to stay with Henry and his mom and not talk to strangers." Donna smoothed the end of the long tail attached to the back of her leggings. "But if everyone is in costume, how will I know if they're a stranger or not?"

Donna had a point. Jamie figured most people would recognize her and Donna, despite Donna's painted-on whiskers and pink nose, and the feathered mask Jamie had added to her own jester's getup. But if someone went all out with a full mask or a furry suit or something, identification might be difficult. "If you're not sure you know someone, ask their name," she said. "If they won't tell you, or you don't recognize the name, walk away. But the best thing is to stay with Henry and Mrs. O'Keefe." Henry's mom had volunteered to chaperone the couple, for which Jamie was deeply grateful. Though she and Donna were attending the charity ball to support those in need, Jamie planned on working, too, trying to spot a killer or killers among the partygoers.

To that end, she'd chosen a costume that allowed her to move, and run if necessary, and that made it easy to conceal her weapon. The multicolored satin tunic, black tights and flat shoes fit the bill perfectly, though she was sure she was in for a night of teasing from her fellow officers. She picked up the jester's hat from the table by the door and handed Donna her coat. "Come on. We don't want to be late."

Volunteers had transformed the Eagle Mountain Community Center into a ballroom that was one part Mardi Gras excess and one part high school prom sentiment. Swaths of black and purple fabric draped the walls and white twinkle lights glowed everywhere. A mirrored disco ball straight out of the 1980s cast spangled light across the dance floor, where a Tyrannosaurus Rex gyrated with a veiled belly dancer and a firefighter in full bunker gear swayed with a woman in a hot pink, retro ski suit.

"Wow!" Donna gasped as she and Jamie waited in line to surrender their tickets.

"Hello, ladies." Adelaide greeted Jamie and Donna when they reached the front of the line. "You both look very nice." Adelaide had teased and sprayed her hair into a 1960s-style beehive and wore oversize hoop earrings and a pink-and-orange paisley minidress.

"What are you supposed to be?" Donna asked.

"I'm a go-go dancer." She stood and lifted one leg to show off orange tights and white, knee-high boots. "Before your time, of course, but I remember those days fondly."

Jamie returned the older woman's grin. She could picture a younger Adelaide grooving to the beat in her psychedelic finery.

They moved farther into the room and surveyed the packed house. Most of the town must have turned out for the fund-raiser. "How are we ever going to find Henry?" Donna asked.

"We'll look for him," Jamie said. "If he's here, we'll find him."

She scanned the milling crowd and spotted Travis right away. No costume and mask could disguise the sheriff's erect form and focused expression. In any case, he was dressed as an Old West lawman, complete with a silver star pinned to a brocaded vest. Next to him his fiancée, Lacy Milligan, looked stunning in a short red-and-black flounced dress that pegged her as an old-time saloon girl.

Gage Walker continued the Old West theme with a mountain man getup, including a fringed buckskin shirt, coonskin cap and what might have been a coyote pelt thrown over one shoulder. The woman in the calico dress, her hair in a prim bun that effectively hid the blue dip-dyed ends, must be his wife, Maya. She was carrying an old-fashioned slate and chalk. Of course. Maya was a schoolmarm—fitting, since she taught at the local high school.

"There's Henry!" Donna jumped up and down and waved enthusiastically at a brown-clad figure hurrying toward them. As he drew nearer, Jamie realized

Henry was dressed as a dog, with floppy ears, whiskers and a shiny black nose.

Mrs. O'Keefe followed him across the floor. A white wig and a cap covered her brown hair, and a dress so wide it must have been held out by a hoopskirt forced her to turn sideways as she maneuvered through the crowd. She held a large plush bone in one hand. "I'm Old Mother Hubbard," she said after they had exchanged greetings. She tapped Henry on the shoulder with the stuffed bone. "This is my poor dog."

Henry paused only a moment to grin at his mother before turning back to Donna. "We want to go get some food," he said.

"All right," Mrs. O'Keefe said. "I'll come with you." She picked up her skirts. "Do you want to come, too?" she asked Jamie.

"Thanks, but I need to check in with the sheriff."

Jamie worked her way through the crowd, past two superheroes, a soldier, three princesses, a witch and many other costumes she couldn't recognize. While she could guess the identity of almost everyone she passed, a knight in full armor and a six-foot rabbit confounded her.

Gage and Maya had moved on by the time Jamie reached Travis and Lacy, and the DJ had turned up the music, so that they had to lean close to hear each other. "Any instructions?" she asked.

"Mingle," Travis said. "Keep an eye on other single women to see if any strangers approach them."

"Stranger is a relative term," Lacy said, scanning

the crowd. "There are some wild costumes. Did you see the guy dressed as an octopus?"

"Just keep your eyes open," Travis said. "And have fun."

Lacy linked her arm in his. "Speaking of fun, I want to check out the silent auction table."

The normally stern sheriff's face transformed as he smiled at Lacy—a smile so full of love and tenderness that it made Jamie's breath catch. What would it be like to have a man look at her that way?

"Hello, Deputy. That's a very amusing costume you have."

She whirled around to find herself face-to-face with a melodrama villain, complete with an outrageously curled black mustache, black suit with a black string tie and a dapper cane. Nate shook one pointed end of her collar, making the attached bell jingle. "Do you know how to juggle?" he asked.

"I do it every day," she deadpanned.

He nodded slowly. "Yes, I guess you do." Leaning on a polished black cane, he looked out at the crowded dance floor. "I'd ask you to dance, but this cast is seriously cramping my style."

She had a sudden memory of dancing with him in a crowded high school gym. They hadn't worried about style back then, content to hold each other close and sway in time to the music. She looked away, afraid the unexpected swell of longing for that time showed on her face. "Don't take this wrong," she said. "But I'm trying to look like I'm at this party alone. Nothing personal."

"Single and vulnerable," he said. "Still trying to lure the killer?"

She shrugged. "It's worth a try."

"What will you do if he takes the bait?"

"I won't let him reel me in, if that's what you're worried about. The idea is to string him along, and find out as much about him as I can."

"Of course, you might just end up with a perfectly innocent man who has a thing for women wearing bells."

She was pretty sure her mask diluted the effect of the scowl she aimed at him, but he got the message. "All right." He held up his hands and took a step back. "I'll see if I can find any tall, sort of masculine women with long blond hair."

He hobbled away into the crowd and Jamie moved toward the buffet table. She caught a glimpse of Donna and Henry on the edge of the dance floor, moving to an upbeat rock song. They made up for their awkwardness with enthusiasm and joy. Donna stood with her hands in the air, swiveling her hips, her tail switching from side to side, while Henry pumped his arms and bent his knees, his puppy-dog ears flopping as he nodded in time to the music. Jamie put a hand to her chest as if she could contain the sudden, fierce swell of love for her sister.

Jamie had been seven when Donna was born. Her parents had explained that Donna was different and would need Jamie's help growing up. But all Jamie had seen was her sister's perfection—her round, dimpled face and trusting brown eyes. As soon as she was able, Donna watched Jamie's every move and tried hard to imitate her big sister. Jamie cheered her on, helped with the exercises and therapy doctors prescribed, played games with her and read to her. Other little girls played with dolls, but Jamie had a real live doll in Donna.

In high school things had changed some, as Jamie grew more independent, working a job, dating, going out with friends and doing so many things that didn't include Donna. And Donna had her own friends, too. She participated in Special Olympics and worked part-time after school. But her sister was always important to her. One of the toughest things about leaving to go to college had been moving away from Donna. Jamie had told herself it would be good for her sister to not be as dependent on her, but she had never hesitated to come home after her parents had died. Donna needed her—and Jamie needed Donna, too. Caring for her sister had helped heal her grief. Donna had given her a purpose and a focus at a time when her life seemed so out of control.

She moved around the room, greeting people she knew, talking briefly, but always moving on. She wanted anyone watching to know that she was here alone, the kind of woman who might be easy prey. After an hour or so she moved on to the buffet table and began filling her plate with food contributed by restaurants in town. She leaned over to snag a mini kebab and jostled a man dressed as a pirate. "Sorry," she said, stepping back.

"Oh, no, ma *cher*. It is *moi* who should apologize."

The French accent was cheesy and obviously fake, but it went with his over-the-top costume—satin-clad pirate, complete with dreadlocks, a fake beard and eye patch. A chill raced up Jamie's spine as she studied him. She was sure she didn't know this guy. She was also sure the costume—and the accent—were designed to hide his identity.

She shifted her plate to her left hand and stuck out her right. "I'm Jamie," she said.

"So charmed, I am sure," he oozed, then bent and kissed her hand. She had to restrain herself from snatching it back, and suppressed a silent *ew*.

Instead, she forced herself to smile and to look at him with what she hoped was a flirtatious expression. "Are you new in town?" she asked. "I don't think I recognize you."

"That is the idea, is it not?" He grinned, revealing a gold tooth—fake, she was sure. It was the kind of thing that might distract a person from looking too closely. But she wasn't distracted. She studied him, searching for any identifying marks. But the wig, beard and eye patch did a good job of hiding most of his features. The one eye that looked back at her was brown, but since that was the most common eye color, the detail might not be significant.

He noticed her studying him and looked away. "I have seen you around town, I think," he said. "Do you live here?"

"Yes. And you?"

"I am a pirate. I live a life of adventure on the high

scas." He turned away and selected a cheese puff from a tray. "Have you tasted these?" he asked. "Delicious."

"Yeah. They look great." She added one to her plate and pretended to survey the rest of the offerings in front of him, while observing him out of the corner of her eye.

"You are here alone?" he asked after a moment.

"Yeah. Uh, my boyfriend and I just split and I've been kind of bummed. But I figure it's time I got back out there and circulated, you know?" Maybe if he thought she was on the rebound, he'd mistake her for an easy mark.

"Ahhh." Hard to interpret that remark. And the fake beard was so full she couldn't tell much about his expression. Had the sheriff or one of her fellow deputies noticed her talking to this guy yet? It wouldn't hurt to have another person she could compare notes with later about his appearance. "Are you here alone?" she asked.

"Yes. Like you, I am all by myself." He set aside his half-eaten food. "Would you like to dance?"

"Sure."

They moved toward the dance floor. When he took her hand, she pretended to look eager, though she couldn't hide her shock when he pulled her so forcefully against him. Still smiling, she pushed back, putting a few inches between them, primarily because she didn't want him to discover that she was armed.

"You do not like me to take liberties," he said, in that same cheesy accent.

"Well, I hardly know you." She forced herself to

smile into his eyes. "Though I wouldn't mind getting to know you better."

"That can be arranged." They swayed together until the song ended, then he led her from the dance floor. "Why don't we go outside, where it's quiet, so we can talk," he said, taking her hand and pulling her toward the door.

The last thing she intended to do was go out into the parking lot with him. She resisted. "I'm having fun," she said. "Let's have another dance." Maybe she could get some of his DNA under her fingernails—scratch him or something. She'd have to make it look like an accident...

"I want to talk, not dance." He pulled her toward the door once more. He was really strong. He wouldn't have had much trouble overpowering the women who were killed, especially with another man helping him.

"Jamie! Jamie! Where are you going?"

Jamie stopped and spun around as Donna jogged up to her. "Where are you going?" Donna asked.

"Nowhere." She pulled free of the pirate's grasp and smoothed Donna's hair. "Are you having a good time?" she asked.

"Yes." Donna looked at the pirate. "Who is this?"

"A friend," the pirate said. He moved as if to take Donna's hand, but Jamie blocked him. The thought of this creep touching her sister made her skin crawl.

"Do you need something?" Jamie asked Donna, pulling her sister's attention away from the pirate.

"I want to go with Henry and his mom back to his

place. She said we could watch a movie and make popcorn. All this noise makes my head hurt."

Jamie glanced over Donna's shoulder and saw Mrs. O'Keefe and Henry approaching. "If it's all right with you, I thought Donna could spend the night," Mrs. O'Keefe said. "We can swing by your house and get her things. She can sleep in the guest room, right across the hall from me. I'll take good care of her."

"Please, Jamie! Please let me go." Donna put her hands together, begging.

"All right," Jamie said. "That sounds like a good idea." A great one, really. Donna would be away from the pirate and his friend and safe, and Jamie would be free to focus on her work.

"Thanks!" Donna kissed Jamie's cheek, then hurried away.

Jamie turned back toward the pirate, but he was gone. She scanned the crowd, searching for him, but he had vanished. Had he left the party—or only gone in search of his next victim?

AFTER MAKING A TOUR of the room and greeting a few people he knew, Nate made a few bids on silent auction items, then filled a plate with food from the buffet and found a chair against one wall. He would have preferred to spend the evening with Jamie. He had looked forward to catching up on all that had been happening in their lives the past four years. He wanted to prove to her that he could be her friend, without demanding more from her than she wanted to give.

Which meant he had to respect this crazy idea she had about putting herself out there as bait for the Ice Cold Killers. No doubt she was capable of looking out for herself, but it wouldn't hurt for him to act as backup, so he made sure to choose a chair that gave him a view of most of the room. He munched chicken wings and cheese balls as she made her way around the room, then stiffened and set aside his plate as a man in a pirate costume started hitting on her. Nate wasn't close enough to hear what the man was saying, but he could read the guy's body language well enough.

When the pirate grabbed Jamie's hand and kissed it, Nate gripped the curved handle of the cane until his knuckles ached. It was made of stout wood and could serve as an effective weapon if need be. He imagined breaking it over the head of this guy, who was standing much too close to Jamie. Who was this joker, to think he could get away with leering at her that way?

Was that the kind of man she wanted—one who leered and kissed her hand, and came on too strong? Was she falling for charm that was as fake as his dreadlocks?

"Do you know him?"

Nate turned to find Travis had taken the chair next to him. The sheriff nodded toward the man with Jamie. "Can you tell who he is under the wig and beard?"

"No." Nate went back to studying the man. The fake beard, mustache, dreadlocks and eye patch covered three-fourths of the man's face. "I don't think I've seen him before."

"Me, either," Travis said. "And Jamie doesn't act as if she recognizes him."

"What makes you think that?" Jamie was smiling at the man now.

"She's leaning away from him," Travis said. "And there's a lot of tension in her shoulders."

Nate saw what Travis meant and felt his own shoulders relax a little. Jamie was flirting with the man, but she wasn't truly attracted to him. She was interested in him as a suspect. "Do you think he's one of the guys you're looking for?" Nate asked, keeping his voice low.

"Maybe," Travis said.

Nate shifted his weight to one hip and slid his phone from his pocket. "Face me and pretend to be posing for a picture," he said. "I'll zoom in for a shot of the pirate."

"Good idea." Travis angled toward Nate, his back to Jamie and the buccaneer. Nate snapped a few photos, zooming in as far as the camera would go. He tucked the phone into his pocket and both men sat back in their chairs again. "I'll send you the files and maybe your tech people can do something with them."

"Thanks," Travis said.

The pirate led Jamie onto the dance floor, where he plastered himself to her. Nate had to grip the edge of his seat to keep from storming out there and prying the two apart. But Jamie put some distance between them and managed the rest of the dance with a pained expression on her face. The song ended and a tug-of-war between the two followed. "I think he's trying to get her to leave," Nate said. He shoved to his feet. "Maybe I need to go interrupt."

Travis put out a restraining hand. "Give it a minute."

Nate stilled but didn't sit back down. Jamie and the pirate continued to argue, and then Donna, Henry and Henry's mother hurried toward her. The pirate stepped back, then began to melt into the crowd.

"I'm going to follow him," Travis said and left.

Donna and the others exited the room and Jamie looked around. Nate hurried toward her, moving as fast as he could with the cane. "I watched the whole thing," he said by way of greeting. "Are you okay?"

"I'm fine." She searched the crowd. "I think he might have been one of the men we're looking for," she said, her voice tight with excitement.

"Travis is following him," Nate said. He touched her shoulder, forcing her to look at him. "What did he say to you?"

"He flirted in this horrible French accent," she said. "In fact, it was so bad, I think that was the point."

"He wanted to disguise his voice," Nate said.

"Yes, I think so."

"After you danced—was he trying to convince you to leave with him?" Nate asked.

"Yes," she said. "But when Donna and the O'Keefes interrupted, he slipped away."

"He didn't want anyone else to see him with you," Nate said.

"I tried to memorize everything I could about him," she said. "But his costume covered up everything. And he didn't have any really outstanding features—no visible moles or a crooked nose or anything."

"I took a few pictures of him with my phone," Nate said. "Travis will have them analyzed. Maybe he can get something from that."

"That was a good idea," Jamie said.

Travis joined them once more, a little breathless. "I lost him," he said. "I saw him slip out the back door to the parking lot, but by the time I made it out there, he was gone."

"Did you get a look at his car?" Nate asked.

Travis shook his head, then turned to Jamie. "What information did he give you?" he asked.

"Not much," she said. "He avoided any of my questions about who he was or where he was from. The costume hid most of his face, and he spoke with a terrible French accent." She sighed. "About all I can tell you is that he has brown eyes, good teeth and is about six feet tall, average build. And he's strong. I think he probably works out. He could have easily overpowered those women."

"I think he's fairly young," Nate said. "He moved like a younger man."

Jamie nodded. "Yes. In his twenties, I think. Maybe early thirties."

"That doesn't give us much to go on," Nate said.

"Send me those photographs you took," Travis said. "We'll print them up and try to find out if anyone else talked to him tonight." He looked around the room. "We'll talk to as many women here as we can tonight. Let's find out if he approached any of them. Maybe they saw or heard something we didn't."

"Adelaide is taking tickets at the door," Jamie said. "She probably saw him when he came in, and she talks to everyone."

"I'll question her," Travis said. "We'll also compare the photograph to the sketches the police artist did from Henry and Tammy's descriptions."

"Were the sketches of the same man?" Nate asked.

"Two different men," Travis said. "If we're right, the man Henry saw with Michaela—the one who called himself Al—is the masked man who came up behind Tammy. The man she described to us is the decoy and accomplice."

They separated to question the other party guests. Though a couple of people Nate talked to had seen the pirate from a distance, none of them had spoken with him. By midnight, the party began breaking up. Nate met up with Travis and Jamie once more. "Adelaide remembers the guy," Travis said. "But she couldn't tell us anything we didn't already know."

"I found one woman he approached," Jamie said. "He asked her to dance, but then her boyfriend returned with a drink and he left in a hurry."

"He doesn't want any witnesses," Travis said. "I'm becoming more and more certain that this is one of the killers." He watched guests file toward the exit. "I don't think there's anything more we can do here tonight. Let's go home, and in the morning we can take a look at the photos Nate took."

He left them. "I'd better get my coat," Jamie said, heading for the cloakroom.

Nate limped alongside her. "Where's Donna?" he asked.

"She's going to spend the night at Henry's house."

"So you're going home alone?"

"I guess I am." A smile ghosted across her lips. "That's something I haven't done in a very long time."

"I'll follow you home," he said.

"You don't have to do that." She accepted her coat—the same down parka she had worn the day he met her and Donna snowshoeing—from the man behind the counter in the cloakroom.

"I know." Nate took the coat and held it for her. "But there's a killer out there who may have been targeting you. I think it's safer if I follow you."

She slipped her arms into the coat, then glanced up at him. "Okay. Thanks."

They fed into the stream of vehicles leaving the community center parking lot, and he followed her to the bungalow on Oak Street. At one time he could have driven to this place blindfolded. He had spent as much time here back in high school as he had in his own house. He parked behind Jamie and followed her to the front door.

"I'll be all right now," she said, as she unlocked the door.

"Humor me and let me make sure," he said.

As soon as she opened the door, the three dogs

galloped toward them, barking furiously when they saw Nate. "Quiet!" Jamie shouted. "It's only Nate."

He had removed the fake mustache in the truck on the way here, along with the hat, so that he hoped he looked more like himself. He bent and offered the back of his hand to the biggest dog—the husky—to sniff. The other dogs followed suit and soon he was patting all three while they jostled for attention.

"They're obviously fine," Jamie said. "They wouldn't act like this if someone had managed to break in."

Nate said nothing, but stumped through all the downstairs rooms, looking for signs of any disturbance. Though, since he didn't live here, how would he know if something was out of place or not, unless the intruder had done something obvious like leave a window open?

"Do you want to look under the bed, too?" she asked, when he returned to her in the foyer, at the bottom of the stairs leading to the second floor.

No, but he wouldn't mind looking *in* her bed. He didn't say the words out loud, but they must have shown on his face. She blushed. She looked so impossibly sweet and sexy. He reached out and removed the jester's hat, and smoothed back her hair.

"What?" she asked.

"Are you sure you'll be okay here tonight, by yourself?" he asked. "If you're nervous, I could stay. I'd sleep on the couch, I promise."

"I'll be fine." She took his arm and led him to the door. "Go home and I'll see you tomorrow at the sheriff's department."

"All right." Maybe he wouldn't go right home. Maybe he'd park his truck down the block and watch her place for a while, just to be sure. She didn't have to know.

He opened the door and started to step onto the porch, but the sight of a dark-colored SUV cruising slowly as it approached made him freeze. "Who's that?" he asked, nodding toward the vehicle.

Jamie peered past him, one hand on his shoulder. "I don't know."

He reached behind her and switched off the porch light, plunging them into shadow. He was aware of her labored breathing as the vehicle drove slowly past. Though the driver was hard to make out in the darkness, Nate was sure he turned his head to look at them.

"The license plate on the car is obscured," Jamie whispered.

Nate pulled her back into the house, and shut and locked the door. "Do you think that was him?" Jamie asked. "The man at the dance?"

"I don't know. It could have been." Nate pulled her close, his heart pounding. He needed to reassure himself that she was safe. She didn't fight him, but relaxed in his embrace, her head nestled in the hollow of his shoulder. "I'm not leaving you here alone," he said.

"No." She lifted her head, her eyes searching his. Then she rose up on tiptoe and pressed her lips to his, her eyes still open, still locked to his.

Chapter Twelve

Nate closed his eyes and gave himself up to the kiss, caressing her with lips and hands, welcoming the tangle of her tongue with his, the soft sweetness of her mouth, the dizzying *want* her touch sent blazing through him.

He didn't know how long it was before she pulled away. He was breathing hard, half wondering if he was dreaming, telling himself he had to keep it together. She had to set the pace here. He had promised himself he wouldn't take more than she would give, and it was a promise he was determined to keep.

"I don't think you should sleep on the couch," she said.

He released his hold on her and took a step back. He couldn't think clearly when she was so close. "Are you sure about this?" he asked, his voice hoarse, not sounding like his own.

She nodded. "I know if I turn my back on these feelings—if I don't give us this chance—then I'm going to regret it."

"Yeah." He raked one hand through his hair.

"Yeah, I'll regret it, too." It felt big and important, a move that would change him—would change them. But it felt right, too.

She leaned past him and double-checked the door lock, then took his hand and led him up the stairs.

JAMIE CLIMBED THE STAIRS, Nate's grip firm and reassuring in hers, helping to calm the butterflies going wild in her chest. She led him down the hall, but not to the room that had been hers growing up. Nate had sneaked up to that room one night, climbing the drainpipe and shimmying across the porch roof to climb into her window. They hadn't really done anything—too fearful of the consequences if they had been caught. But there had been something so thrilling about cuddling together on her bed—she in flannel pajamas decorated with pink hearts, he in jeans and a sweatshirt. They had kissed and whispered to each other until, hearing her father get up to go to the bathroom and sure his next stop would be her bedroom, he had slipped out the window and to the ground once more.

But she didn't take him to that room. About a year after her parents' death, she had moved into the master bedroom. She had given away their king-size bed and replaced it with an iron four-poster she had purchased from a local antique shop, making payments each pay period for three months until the bed was hers. She had stored the family photos that had adorned the walls and replaced them with black-and-white photos of Eagle Mountain landscapes, also purchased from a local shop.

Nate stopped in the doorway and surveyed the room. "What?" she asked. "Are you weirded out because this used to be my parents' room?"

"No. I'd forgotten this was theirs. I was just admiring it. Admiring you."

"You were looking at the walls—you weren't looking at me."

"I was admiring what the walls tell me about you."

She faced him, hands on his shoulders. "What do they tell you?"

His eyes met hers. "That you love beautiful things. Not frilly or over the top, but beautiful." He tossed the cane aside and fit his hands to her waist. "That you love this place—you love Eagle Mountain."

"I do," she said. That was one of the things that made her so uneasy about him. Nate had come back to Eagle Mountain, but she didn't sense that it was home for him—not the way it was home for her.

But she didn't want to think about that now. And she didn't want to talk anymore. When he opened his mouth as if to speak, she put two fingers to his lips to silence him, then she began loosening the knot of his string tie.

Tie loosened, she began working her way down the buttons on his starched white shirt. He slid his hand around to lower the zipper on her tunic, the sudden rush of cool air on her back mitigated by his warm hand smoothing down her spine. Impatient to be closer still, she pushed his jacket off his shoulders, then his shirt, her heart thudding harder as she admired the defined muscles of his chest and shoulders.

Stripped of camouflaging clothing, he resembled a Viking warrior.

"Your turn," he murmured and pushed the tunic over her shoulders and down to the floor, followed quickly by the tights, until she was standing before him in her bra and panties, goose bumps prickling her arms and shoulders. He stripped out of his trousers and stood before her in boxers—which did little to hide his desire. She was contemplating this, dry mouthed and breathless, when he forced her attention to more practical concerns. "What about protection?" he asked.

"In the drawer by the bed."

He moved the short distance to the bed, opened the drawer of the nightstand and took out a package of condoms, and gave her a questioning look.

"Don't flatter yourself," she said, her face burning.

"I didn't say anything."

"You didn't have to—I could see it in your eyes." She joined him by the bed. "You thought I bought these, planning to bring you up here."

"It's none of my business why you bought them," he said. "I'm just glad you have them." He sat on the side of the bed and began to open the package.

But she couldn't not tell him now. "There was this guy I went out with a few times. I thought maybe…" She shook her head. "Nothing came of it." She pressed her lips together. She had said enough. She didn't want him to know there hadn't been anyone else since him. She hadn't dated much, what with Donna and her job. And when she did go out with someone, she found it difficult to let down her guard with men.

He set aside the condom box and reached for her. "It's okay. Come here."

She crawled onto the bed next to him, nerves warring with excitement. She wanted this—needed this. But she was afraid of making a mistake.

Then he was kissing her, hands gently exploring, warm fingers coaxing delicious sensations from her. She began to relax and to make her own discoveries about his body. Everything about him—about being here with him—was both familiar and new. He was Nate—the first man and the only man she had ever made love with. The man she had trusted with all her secrets. He was the same—yet very different. He was bigger than she remembered. Broader and more muscular. A man, where he had been a boy.

"You've grown into a beautiful woman," he said, shaping his hand to one breast.

"I guess we've both changed," she said, breathless again as he dragged his thumb across her sensitive nipple.

"For the better." He kissed her fiercely, his hand moving down to stroke her sex, until desire all but overwhelmed her. She felt impatient, desperate and a little out of control.

"I really don't want to wait anymore," she said, digging her fingers into the taut skin of his shoulders.

In answer, he held her close and plunged two fingers into her, then began to stroke more deftly. She came fast and hard, thrusting against him, crying out in relief. He held her a little while longer and then, smiling, he reached for the box of condoms.

When they came together again, she felt more in control, though no less eager for him. As he filled her she let out a long sigh that grew to a low moan as he began to move. Nervousness long vanquished, she matched his rhythm, every sense focused on the moment. Desire began to build once more, lifting her up, climbing with him to that wonderful height. When at last she could wait no longer and leaped, he followed, the two of them clinging tightly together for the glide back down to earth.

Neither of them said anything for long minutes. She rested her head on his chest and reveled in the strong, steady thud of his heartbeat, and the rise and fall of his body beneath hers with each breath. She felt so connected to him it took all her strength to shove off the bed and head to the bathroom.

When she returned a few moments later, she thought from the steady, deep rhythm of his breathing that he was asleep. She slid in next to him and he reached for her. "I was afraid for you tonight," he said.

It took her a moment to comprehend that he was talking about earlier in the evening, when the pirate had approached her. "I was never in any danger," she said.

"I know. But if that was one of the killers—he's murdered six women, seemingly at random. Someone with a mind like that—it's terrifying."

"Yes, it is." She propped herself on one elbow,

wanting to see his face. "Thank you for following me home and for offering to stay."

"You would have sent me away, if we hadn't seen that car driving past."

"I would have regretted it. I might even have called you back before you got to your truck."

He laughed and pulled her close in a bear hug. "I was going to park my truck at the end of the block and watch your house all night, to make sure you were safe."

The words brought a lump to her throat. To think that he cared so much. Fearing losing control, she rolled onto her back and searched for a less emotional topic of conversation. "How is your ankle?" she asked.

"Sex is a terrific pain reliever." He lay back beside her. "I figure in another week or so I'll be able to ditch the cane."

"I'm glad it's not bothering you too much."

"The worst part is the boredom. I haven't been off work this long since I graduated college. I used to think I was lazy, but I've discovered I really hate being idle."

"Me, too." She laughed. "Though sometimes I think it might be nice to try out a life of leisure—for a few days, anyway."

He reached down and laced his fingers in her hand. "You've got a lot on your plate. Tell me about Donna."

The question surprised her. It wasn't as if Nate hadn't known Donna almost as long as he had known Jamie. "What about her?"

"She seems to have things together and is pretty smart. Will she ever be able to live on her own?"

Jamie tensed and took her hand from his. Why was he asking that question? Why now? "Maybe. But she'll always need help. The man I end up with has to take Donna as part of the bargain." Might as well be up-front about that now. She held her breath, waiting for his answer.

"Of course," he said. "I like Donna. I always have. It's good to see her so happy."

She relaxed again. He wasn't lying. His acceptance and even affection for Donna was one of the reasons she had fallen in love with him. "I hope she does okay tonight. She's never spent a night away from home before. She's never wanted to."

"And it feels strange to you," he said.

"Yes. But everything about this night is a little strange."

"You didn't think I'd be here with you."

"No. But I'm glad you are." She took his hand again.

He rolled over to face her and pulled her close once more. "I'm always here for you," he said. "I'm going to keep saying that until you believe it."

She believed he meant his words, but she didn't trust him not to break his own promise. She owed it to herself not to let him break her heart, too.

NATE LEFT JAMIE'S place after breakfast the next morning. She didn't come right out and say so, but he sensed she wanted him gone before her sister returned home. He could understand explaining his presence might be awkward, and he was willing to let her ease into the idea of the two of them being together again.

He headed toward the sheriff's department, and along the way found himself searching driveways and side streets for the dark SUV that had driven past Jamie's house the night before. Had the driver really been the man in the pirate costume—the murderer? Or had he and Jamie let paranoia and fear get the better of them? In broad daylight, it was easy to think the latter, but he decided to reserve judgment until after he talked to the sheriff.

Travis was at his desk and hard at work. Upcoming wedding or not, the sheriff was going to spend every spare hour on this case.

"Any luck getting an ID from the photo I sent, or the police artist sketches?" Nate asked, after Adelaide had escorted him to Travis's office.

"No." Travis passed a sheet of paper to Nate. "Take a look."

The paper featured side-by-side comparisons of the photograph Nate had taken of the pirate and two sketches of men. "Are these the police artist sketches from the information Henry and Tammy provided?" Nate asked.

"Yes. Do either of them look familiar to you?"

Nate studied the images, comparing each to the photograph of the pirate, and to his mental images of people he knew. "I don't recognize them," he said. "And neither of them looks like the pirate to me."

"The police artist thinks the guy in the pirate costume may have made his nose look larger with makeup, and the gold tooth is probably a fake," Travis said. "He suggested we look for someone with a theatrical background, so I asked the local theatre group to give me a list of any men who have been involved in their productions." He passed Nate a second sheet of paper. "I've highlighted the names of men who fall into the right age group. There are only half a dozen."

Nate's eyebrows rose. "Gage's name is on here."

"Yeah. He was in a comedy revue they did a couple of years ago. I left it on there to give him a hard time, but he was with me when several of the murders occurred, so we can safely rule him out."

Nate tossed the papers back onto the desk and lowered himself into the visitor's chair. "Last night, I followed Jamie home from the community center," he said. "I was worried about her being alone. I know she's a cop, but these two killers seem to have a knack for eluding us."

"Never a bad idea to be safe," Travis said.

"Yeah, well, I was saying goodnight to her when a dark-colored SUV passed. It could have been dark gray or black, and I think it was a Toyota. It passed the house very slowly, and it seemed the driver was looking at the house—though it was dark, so I can't be sure." He gripped the arms of the chair and leaned toward Travis. "The license plate was obscured—the license plate light was out and it looked as if mud or something else had been smeared over most of the plate."

"Whoever was driving the car didn't want the plate read," Travis said. "What did you do?"

"We decided I should spend the night at her place, in case the guy came back." He kept his expression blank, letting Travis use his imagination to fill in any details on sleeping arrangements. No way was Nate going to elaborate. Travis was his friend, but he was also Jamie's boss, and there were some things he didn't need to know.

"I'll add your description of the vehicle to the other information we've collected," Travis said.

Nate sat back again, frustration churning his stomach. "What's your gut tell you on this?" he asked. Travis would have made it his business to know everything there was to know about this case, and he was good at spotting patterns and making connections.

Travis drew in a deep breath and waited a long beat before he spoke. "We're looking for two men—young and strong, from five-nine to, say, six-two," he said. "They're working together. One of them can pass as a woman while wearing a wig, and probably acted as a decoy to induce the victim to stop, so that the other man could overpower her. That decoy technique may be a new twist or something they've done all along."

"You know most of the people around here," Nate said. "Do you have any suspects in mind?"

"There were two men who were on my radar from the very first," he said. "College students who were here over winter break. My sister invited them to the scavenger hunt at the ranch where Fiona Winslow was killed."

"I think I remember them," Nate said. "Cocky young guys. They got in an argument with Fiona and Ken Rutledge."

"Right. They may have been the last to see Fiona before she left Ken and went looking for a couple of the other women."

"You said they were on your radar? But no longer?"

"They supposedly left town when the road reopened briefly earlier in the month. At least, I haven't seen them around, and they moved out of the cabin where they were staying."

"But they could still be here," Nate said. "Hiding."

"They could."

"I assume you contacted the school they attend?"

"I did. Neither of them reported for classes. But they could have decided to quit school."

"What about parents? Friends?"

"I don't have that information," Travis said. "The aunt who owns the cabin here where they were staying hasn't heard from them. If the roads were open, I'd send someone to Fort Collins to talk to people. I contacted a local investigator and asked him to do some checking, but we don't have much of a budget for that kind of thing, and so far he hasn't come up with anything significant. No one can say for sure these two are in Fort Collins—but no one is sure they aren't, either."

"I've got lots of time on my hands," Nate said. "I

could drive around the county, do some checking. Tell me who I'm looking for. I sort of remember them from before, but not clearly."

"I'll print out their ID photos for you. Their names are Alex Woodruff and Tim Dawson."

"Alex. That could be the Al who was with Michaela," Nate said.

"Maybe. Tammy and Henry are coming in this morning to look at some photographs, including the one you took last night. We'll see if they can pick out Alex and Tim."

"I have a few ideas of places they might be staying," Nate said.

"Tell me, and I'll send a couple of deputies out to check," Travis said.

Nate shook his head. "I want to look around first before you waste any of your resources. I'll let you know if I see anything suspicious."

"If you find these two, call for backup," Travis said. "After what they did to these women, they won't think twice about killing you."

"I'm no hero," Nate said. "If we find them, we'll send in our own army to take them. They won't know what hit them."

"The women they killed probably didn't, either," Travis said. "I want to make it tougher for them to take anyone by surprise, so I'm holding a press conference at eleven. I'm going to let everyone know about the possible use of a decoy, as well as release the photograph of the pirate and the two police sketches. Maybe we'll get lucky and someone knows where these two are hiding."

"What about releasing the photos of Tim and Alex?" Nate asked. "That's probably your best bet of finding out if anyone around here has seen them lately."

"I may do that, too." The printer that sat on the credenza behind Travis whirred and he leaned back and plucked a sheet of paper from the tray. "These are Alex Woodruff and Tim Dawson's driver's license photos," he said as he handed the printout to Nate.

Nate studied the photos of the two young men— one with straight, sandy hair cut short, the other with a mop of brown curls. His eyes widened and his heart beat faster. "I know these guys." He looked up and met the sheriff's gaze. "They're definitely still in the area. I talked to them only four days ago."

Chapter Thirteen

Donna returned from her stay with the O'Keefes full of descriptions of what she saw, what they ate and everything she had done. Jamie listened to this nonstop narrative as she cleaned up the kitchen, delighted the evening had gone so well—and only a little guilty that she had scarcely missed her sister, focused as she was on Nate. Donna, so caught up in her own happy memories, never asked how Jamie had spent her evening.

At nine forty-five, she and Donna loaded all three dogs into the car for their annual checkups. Darcy Marsh was the newest veterinarian in town, a pleasant young woman who had a real rapport with animals. She greeted Donna, Jamie and the three dogs enthusiastically. "I saw you at the masquerade last night but never made my way around to you," she said, as she washed her hands before examining the dogs.

"I'm sorry I missed you," Jamie said.

"What was your costume?" Donna asked. "I was a cat."

"You were a very cute cat," Darcy said. "Ryder and I went as Roy Rogers and Dale Evans—complete with stick horses." She laughed. "At least they raised a lot of money to help people who have been hurt by the road closures. And we had a lot of fun."

"How is Ryder?" Jamie asked. Darcy's fiancé, Ryder Stewart, was a Colorado State Highway Patrol trooper.

"He's great." Darcy put her stethoscope to Targa's chest and for a few moments, the only sound in the room was the dogs panting loudly. "She sounds good," Darcy pronounced at last. "Now let's hear the rest of them."

Some fifteen minutes later, after Darcy had examined ears, teeth and every other accessible part of the three dogs, she pronounced all the canines in good health. While Jamie paid the bill, Donna and a vet tech took the dogs out to Jamie's SUV. "At the party last night, did either of you notice a guy dressed as a pirate?" Jamie asked Darcy and her receptionist, Stacy. "He had long dreadlocks, a beard and mustache and an eye patch, and he spoke with a cheesy French accent."

"I didn't see anybody like that," Stacy said as she accepted Jamie's credit card.

"Me, either." Darcy leaned toward Jamie. "Why do you ask?"

Jamie shook her head. "I was just wondering."

But Darcy wasn't going to be put off so easily. "Are you working on this Ice Cold Killer case?" she asked.

"I think it's safe to say every law enforcement officer in the county is working on this case," Jamie hedged.

"Yeah. But the sheriff's department would know

more than anyone." Darcy rubbed her arms, as if she was chilled. "I just wondered if you're any closer to finding out who is killing all these women. I'm still trying to wrap my head around Kelly being gone."

Kelly Farrow had been Darcy's partner in the veterinary business—and the Ice Cold Killer's first victim. Had that really been less than a month ago?

"We have some leads," Jamie said. "I can't say anything more, but it feels like we're making progress."

"Thanks," Darcy said. "That helps a little, I guess."

It didn't really help, Jamie knew. Nothing would until the killings stopped. Even she, with all her law enforcement training, didn't feel safe alone anymore. She signed the credit card slip, said goodbye, then headed across the parking lot to where Donna and the dogs waited in the SUV. Jamie stopped short, her hand on the door handle, as a dark SUV pulled out of the lot. The hairs on the back of her neck stood up as she tried to read the vehicle's license plate and realized it was obscured.

Heart racing, she yanked open her car door and slid into the driver's seat. She started the engine with one hand and fastened her seat belt with the other, then took off out of the parking lot, tires squealing.

"Why are you driving so fast?" Donna asked, steadying herself with one hand on the dashboard.

"I thought I saw someone I know and I want to catch up with him," Jamie said. She scanned the road ahead and the driveways they passed, but there was no sign of the SUV.

"Who are you trying to find?" Donna asked.

"A man I met at the party last night."

"The pirate? Henry and I saw you talking to him." Donna shook her head. "He didn't look very nice to me."

For all her innocence and tendency to be too trusting, Donna sometimes had very good instincts about people. "I don't think he is very nice," Jamie said. "If you see him again, don't say anything to him, just come find me. If you're at work, you can call me."

"Is he a bad man?" Donna sank down in her seat, her face creased with worry.

"I don't know," Jamie said. "But you remember we talked about this before. It's good to be careful around people you don't know."

"I know."

Jamie pulled into the parking lot of the history museum and turned the SUV around. "Let's go home," she said. "We both need to get ready for work." She would tell the sheriff about the dark SUV with the obscured plate. They'd have a better chance of finding it if everyone in the department was looking. The killer had been able to hide from them so far, but as long as the roads stayed closed, he wouldn't be able to run far.

"I MET THESE two while I was on patrol Tuesday." Nate tapped the photos Travis had given him. "They were ice climbing that exposed rock face by Snowberry campground. I'm sure it was the same two, though they introduced themselves as Lex and Ty. I even thought they looked familiar, but I didn't connect them to the scavenger hunt at your ranch."

"Did they say anything to indicate where they were staying?" Travis grabbed a notepad and prepared to take notes.

"No. But they did tell me they were college graduates. They shut down my attempts to get any more information." Nate grimaced. "I stopped to ask them if they'd seen a woman with long blond hair in the area. They said no, but they mentioned the Ice Cold Killer. They seemed eager to talk about it, in fact."

"Oh? What did they say?"

"Mainly, they talked about how good the killer was at eluding you. Their exact words were that the killer was making you look like an idiot."

Travis nodded. "That fits with the suggestion we've had that the killer likes taunting law enforcement. He wants to prove he's smarter than the people who are pursuing him." He pushed his chair back. "I'm going to put out an APB on these guys, and I'll mention them at my press conference this morning. If they're in the area, someone will see them and we'll find them."

"Let me know if I can do anything to help," Nate said.

He left the sheriff's department, but instead of going home, he headed to the national forest, to the campground where he had encountered Alex and Tim. He parked at the entrance to the closed campground and walked over to the rock wall where the two had been climbing. A cold wind buffeted him as he got out of the truck. A low, gray sky promised more snow soon. The drifts at the foot of the wall lay undisturbed. Leaning heavily on his crutch, Nate scanned the area for any trace the two might have left behind. They had been meticulous about cleaning up their crime scenes, but they might not have been so careful here.

But any evidence they might have left had been buried by four inches of fresh snow. Nate returned to his truck and sat, thinking. The two young men had abandoned their aunt's cabin, perhaps because they sensed the sheriff was closing in on them. Though they had had a chance to leave town when the road opened briefly, they had elected to stick around and continue the killings. Three women had been murdered since the road had closed again. Alex and Tim had to be living somewhere. Somewhere without neighbors who might get suspicious and report them to the sheriff's department. Somewhere near here—the area where the murder of Michaela Underwood and the attack on Tammy Patterson had occurred.

Of course! He slapped the steering wheel, then started the truck. Why hadn't he seen it before? The squatters in the summer cabin—the ones who had set those animal traps around the hideout—they had to be Alex and Tim.

He drove to the cabin and parked past the cabins, at a trailhead that was little used this time of year, then hiked back to the cabins. At the chain across the road, he unholstered his weapon and took a firmer grip on his cane. He didn't intend to confront anyone who might be here, but he wanted to be prepared in case they spotted him first.

The snow on the road leading to the cabins had been packed down by the sheriff's department vehicles, making walking less arduous than the last time Nate was here. He paused halfway up to take in the scattering of cabins, each a short distance from its neighbor, with its own picnic table and outbuildings. In summer, these cabins would form a thriving community. The same families had owned these little getaways for generations, and each summer would be a reunion of old friends. Grandparents and grandchildren, parents who had come here as children themselves and new people who had married into the families would gather for barbecue and picnics, volleyball games and horseshoe competitions. With no cell phone or television service, and little space inside the small dwellings, they looked to each other and the outdoors for entertainment. Cherished memories and soul-deep relationships kept families returning year after year, and made them guard jealously what was, for many, a little piece of heaven.

In the cold of winter the cabins didn't look so inviting. They stood with shuttered windows and padlocked doors in the ringing silence of the forest, like a forgotten ghost town. Nate moved silently through the deep snow, a wraith himself, slipping between the trees.

Alert for any sign of more traps, he approached the cabins slowly, moving as stealthily as possible, hampered as he was by the crutch and the awkward air boot. He reached the cabin the traps had been taken from first. He could see them piled on the front porch, and the pale outlines where they had hung on the side of the building.

He passed the other six cabins, pausing to scan the snow around each one for any sign of activity before moving on to the cabin where he had been snared. There were more signs of activity here—depressions covered over by fresh snow that marked the path of law enforcement vehicles in and out, churned earth where he had sat waiting for rescue, and new, stout padlocks on the front and back doors.

Nate stood on the back porch of the cabin, searching through the trees. Though this cabin was the furthest back in the grouping, the forest road looped around behind it, so that anyone sitting on this porch, or looking out the back picture window, could hear approaching traffic, and even catch a glimpse of the vehicle through a gap in the trees.

Nate studied that gap, then started walking, making his way through the trees until he reached an opening that widened out to provide access to the road. Someone could park a vehicle here, access it via the path through the woods, and be gone before anyone driving on the road reached the cabin.

At the sound of an approaching vehicle, he shrank back into the trees, and watched as a Rayford County sheriff's department vehicle sped by. Grinning, Nate made his way back to the cabin.

He was waiting on the front porch when Travis and

Gage pulled in. "Where's your truck?" Travis asked as he mounted the steps.

"I parked at a trailhead down the road," Nate said.

"That's a long way to walk with a busted ankle," Gage said.

"I didn't want anyone to see me."

"Whereas, we didn't care." Gage looked around them. "I guess you had the same idea we did."

"Alex and Tim must have been the squatters in this cabin," Nate said.

"It's a good place to hide," Gage said. "But they risked being trapped in here. There's only one entrance or exit."

"Not exactly." Nate stood. "Let me show you what I found." He led them back through the woods to the clearing next to the road. "If they kept a lookout, they could be out of the cabin and gone before law enforcement reached them," he said.

"They could even set up an alarm to warn them when someone was coming," Gage said as the three of them walked back to the cabin. "One of those cables you drive over and it rings a bell or something. Or a camera focused on the drive."

"We didn't find anything like that when we searched the place," Travis said.

"It's like the crime scenes," Gage said. "They know how to clean up after themselves."

"We're going to look again." Travis paused at the door and pulled on a pair of gloves. "You can help if you want, Nate."

"Sure." He accepted a pair of gloves. "It's not as if I have anything better to do."

An hour later they had combed every inch of the small cabin and come up with nothing to link Alex and Tim to either the cabin or the murders.

"They've cleared out of here," Travis said. "We'll check the other cabins, but I don't think we'll find anything."

"I walked around all of them when I arrived today," Nate said. "I didn't find any sign of activity at any of them."

"There are more of these summer cabins, aren't there?" Gage asked.

"There's one more grouping like this, with six cabins, on the other side of the county," Nate said.

"Then that's where we look next," Travis said.

"Let me go with you," Nate said.

Travis looked at the cast boot on his leg.

"I'll stay out of the action," Nate said. "I won't get in your way. But you need me there."

"Why is that?" Gage asked.

"Because I have a key to the gate," Nate said. "I can get you in there without anyone else knowing."

Chapter Fourteen

When Jamie arrived for her shift Saturday afternoon, Nate met her in the hallway. He had shed the cast boot and traded the crutch for a cane, which recalled the costume he had worn last night—and everything else about last night. But Jamie was pretty sure he could have greeted her dressed as a clown and she would have still thought about last night. "Hello," he said, the warmth in his smile making her heart beat a little faster.

"Hi." She nodded and started to move past him, determined to remain professional while she was on the job.

He turned and walked alongside her. "Busy morning?" he asked.

"Uh, yeah. We took the dogs to the vet." Should she mention the dark SUV she had seen pulling out of the lot?

"Did you catch the sheriff's press conference this morning?" Nate asked.

"No. I didn't know there was one." Was she supposed to have been there? No one had notified her. "What was it about?"

"He'll fill you in. There's a meeting in five minutes."

"I saw the notice in the locker room." Maybe she would bring up the SUV in the meeting.

Jamie and Nate were the last to enter the situation room, where Travis stood at the end of the conference table, beside a large poster on an easel. The poster featured the enlarged photos of two young men, two sketches of men and a photograph of the man dressed in the pirate costume.

"For those of you who might not have heard the press conference this morning, these are two men we want to question regarding the Ice Cold Killer murders." Travis indicated the left photo, of a slender young man with light brown hair. "This is Alex Woodruff, also known as Al, also known as Lex. He may be using other names." Travis consulted his notes. "He's twenty-two years old, until recently an undergraduate at Colorado State University, where he was studying psychology. He was also involved in the university's theatrical company, where he met Tim Dawson."

Travis indicated the second photograph, of a young man with dark, curly hair. "Tim, also known as Ty, is twenty-one, also a psych major, also active in the theatre company. As far as I have been able to determine, the two did not return to classes when they started up again last week. Previously they were staying in a cabin belonging to Tim's aunt, on County Road Five.

They left there some time before last week and may have broken into and been living at Sundance cabins, though they are no longer there."

Jamie and several others at the table looked at Nate. "Yeah, that's the cabin where I was hurt," he said.

"Alex and Tim may have set those traps to slow down anyone who came after them," Travis said. "Nate talked to them that morning near Snowberry campground. They were climbing, and introduced themselves as Lex and Ty."

"They're not very creative with their aliases," Gage observed.

"They were driving a dark gray Toyota High-lander," Nate said. "I made note of the license plate and the vehicle is registered to Timothy Dawson."

"Alex Woodruff and Tim Dawson were suspects for the first three murders," Travis said. "We ruled them out after they supposedly left town. Now that we know they're back in town, we need to bring them in and question them."

He tapped the drawings in the middle of the poster. "These are drawings the police artist from Denver made after Skype sessions with Henry O'Keefe and Tammy Patterson. As you can see, they bear some re-semblance to Alex and Tim, though nothing definitive. We brought Henry and Tammy back in this morning, and Henry picked out Alex's photo from a selection of photos we gave him, and identified him as the man he saw with Michaela Underwood the day before she was murdered. Tomorrow we'll take the photo to the bank and see if any of Michaela's coworkers recognize him. Tammy wasn't able to identify the man who was posing as a woman who lured her to stop, probably because of his disguise."

Travis moved on to the photograph at the bottom of the poster. "This man was at the masquerade party at the community center last night," he said. "He approached Deputy Douglas and tried to persuade her to come into the parking lot with him. When they were interrupted, he fled. He could be Alex or Tim in disguise, but we can't be sure."

He laid aside the pointer and faced them. "I've released these images to the media, and I've issued a BOLO for Alex, Tim and their vehicle. We're hoping someone will spot them and report the sighting."

"In the meantime, we're going to keep hunting for them. Dwight, I want you and Jamie to come with me and Gage this afternoon. We're going to check another set of summer cabins. These two have to be living somewhere, and since they broke into one cabin, they might try another."

He looked around the table. "Does anyone else have any questions, or anything to add?"

Jamie raised her hand.

"Yes, Deputy?"

"This morning, as I was leaving Darcy Marsh's veterinarian office, I saw a dark gray SUV, with the license plate obscured, exiting the parking lot."

"Do you think this was the same vehicle that drove by your house last night?" Travis asked.

Jamie stared. How had Travis known about that vehicle?

He must have read the question on her face. "Nate mentioned a vehicle fitting that description drove slowly past your house late last night," he said.

Nate! What else had he told his buddy, Travis, about last night? She tried hard to fight back a blush but wasn't sure she succeeded. "Yes, I think it was the same vehicle," she said. "A dark gray SUV—it could have been a Highlander—with the license plate obscured."

"We'll add that information to what we already know," Travis said.

She sat back, avoiding looking at Nate—or at anyone else. If the sheriff knew about her and Nate, how long would it be before everyone knew? Not that she was ashamed of having him spend the night, but she liked to keep her private life private. She didn't want to be the subject of gossip.

As soon as the meeting was over, she stood and made for the door. But Nate waylaid her in the hallway. "Jamie, wait up!" he called. "I'll ride with you to the cabins."

She pretended she hadn't heard, but that only made Nate raise his voice. "Jamie!"

She whirled to face him. "What?"

The word came out louder than she had intended. Now everyone was staring. She wished a hole would open in the floor and she could drop down into it.

Nate clomped up to her. "What's wrong?" he asked. "You look upset."

Aware of the others around them, she made for an empty office. Nate followed and shut the door behind him. If any of the others had seen them come in here—and they probably had, because cops didn't miss much—they'd talk. But at least what they said would only be speculation. "Did you tell Travis you were at my house last night?" she asked.

"Yes," Nate said. "He needed to know about the SUV we saw. It could be important to the case."

"Did you tell him you spent the night?"

"Yes."

She wanted to shake him but settled for clenching her hands. "Nate, how could you? He's my boss."

"I told him I stayed in case the guy in the pirate costume decided to pay you a visit. For all he knows, I slept on the couch." He put his hands on her shoulders. "I respect your privacy," he said. "And I'm not the kind of guy who shares private details like that with anyone else."

"Travis is your friend."

"Yes, but like you said, he's your boss. I'm not going to talk about you with him. It wouldn't be right."

She had never known Nate to lie to her before. Some of the tension in her shoulders eased. "Thank you. I'm sorry I overreacted. I just…" She shook her head.

"You want to take things slow," he said. "I understand. But remember—we're both single. We don't work for the same department. There's nothing wrong with us having a relationship."

"I know." She reached up and caressed his forearm. "But this is all so new…"

He kissed her forehead. "I know. You want to be sure this is going to work for you before you say anything. I get that. And I can be patient."

"Thanks for understanding." She wanted to melt into his arms and enjoy more than that gentle peck on the forehead. But she was on the clock, and they both had work to do. "Come on," she said. "We'd better get going."

The Juniper Creek cabins were tucked alongside a frozen creek in a section of national forest up against the base of Dakota Ridge. Since Nate was riding with her, Jamie ended up leading the convoy of sheriff's office vehicles. She stopped at the pipe gate that blocked the entrance to the cabins and Nate got out and postholed through the snow to unlock one of half a dozen padlocks affixed to the chain around the gatepost.

"Why do you have a key?" she asked, when he returned to the cruiser.

"A buddy of mine owns one of the cabins. He lives in Denver now, so he gave me a key so I could check on the place for him."

As Travis had instructed, Jamie parked in the road at the bottom of a hill that led up to the cabins. The other deputies and the sheriff arranged their vehicles around hers to form a barricade across the road. Then they got out and gathered around the sheriff.

"We'll pair up and search every cabin for any signs of recent occupation," Travis said. "Nate will wait here and radio if anyone approaches. If you see anyone, or anything that raises concern, radio for backup. And be very cautious. They set a booby trap at the other cabin, so it's likely, if they've moved here, they've done the same."

Jamie and Deputy Dwight Prentice were tasked with searching the first three cabins. Six little residences formed a semicircle at the top of a rise, identical square cottages with front and back porches, metal roofs and board-and-batten siding painted forest service green. Heavy wooden shutters covered the windows, and stovepipes protruded from most of the roofs.

They approached up the road. As Jamie followed Dwight, trying to walk in the tracks he left in the deep snow, she was uncomfortably aware that anyone at the top of that hill would be able to see them coming. Though they all wore ballistic vests, a shooter could still do a lot of damage, and even kill them.

But no one fired on them, and the only sounds were the movements of the other members of the sheriff's department. "It doesn't look like anyone has come this way in a while," Dwight said when they reached the first cabin. A set of elk antlers hung over the front door, and a breeze stirred wind chimes that hung from one corner of the eaves.

Dwight tried the door, then knocked. "Sheriff's department!" he called loudly. "Open up!"

No one answered. She and Dwight hadn't expected them to. A stout padlock secured the front door. But they had to follow procedure.

Jamie peered through a gap in the shutters over the

big front window, but could make out nothing in the darkness. "Let's check the perimeter," Dwight said.

They each circled around one side of the structure and met at the steps leading up to the rear porch, which had been screened in. The screen door was open, revealing a patio table and a stack of lawn chairs. The back door into the house was locked.

"Let's check the other cabins," Jamie said.

She led the way this time to the second cabin in the circle. The front door of this one featured a hand-carved wooden sign identifying it as McBride's Place. Snow had drifted around the foundation and buried the back steps. As with the first cabin, Dwight and Jamie found no sign that anyone had been here in weeks.

They had the same results at the third cabin. To Jamie, the whole enclave felt deserted, preserved under a blanket of snow, waiting for spring. If Alex and Tim had ever been here, they had moved on before the last big snow.

They met Gage and Travis in front of the sixth cabin, and walked together back along the road toward the vehicles. "We didn't see any sign that anyone has been here," Dwight reported.

"Some here," Gage said. He scanned the thick woods around them. "It's a good hiding place, but maybe too remote for our killers. The other cabins were closer to town and other people."

"None of the murders have occurred near here," Travis said. "But they have to have shelter. We chased them out of the other cabin, so where did they go?"

"Maybe they have a friend who's putting them up," Jamie said.

"Or they broke into a summer home," Dwight said. "There are plenty of those in the area."

Travis nodded, but said nothing.

Nate met them at the gate. "Did you find anything?" he asked.

"Nothing," Travis said. "You should have waited in the cruiser. It would have been warmer."

"I've been doing some investigating of my own," Nate said. "I can't let you have all the fun."

"What did you find?" Travis asked.

"It might be nothing. Then again, it might be something." He led them back through the gate, up the Forest Service road about fifty feet to a trailhead. "I started thinking," Nate said. "This trail runs along behind the cabins, on the other side of the creek. It might be a back way in. And someone's used it recently." He indicated tracks from snowshoes. "Two people, as close as I can figure."

"But we didn't find any tracks by the cabins," Gage said. "Unless someone is flying in through a window, we'd have seen signs of their passage in the snow."

"It could just be recreational snowshoers," Dwight said.

"It could," Nate agreed. "I still think it's worth following them, at least until you're past the cabins."

"Dwight and I can check them out," Jamie said.

"All right," Travis said. "We'll wait at the vehicles."

Jamie and Dwight headed up the trail. The snow was soft, which made the going slow. Deeper in the woods, the snowshoe tracks were more clearly visible, oval outlines in the snow. "I'd guess two men, from the size of the tracks," Dwight said.

"Yeah," Jamie said. "And it probably is just a couple of guys out for the day. We know no one went near the cabins."

"The killers have done a pretty good job of staying one step ahead of us," Dwight said. "If they were the ones at the Sundance cabins, they might have figured we'd look here next—it's a similar setup."

"Maybe," Jamie said. "But it doesn't hurt to check." When they had traveled about a quarter of a mile up the trail, she glimpsed one of the cabins through the trees. "If someone was going to cut over to the cabins, they'd do it somewhere in here," she said.

"Right here." Dwight stopped and indicated where the tracks turned off.

Picking up their pace, Dwight and Jamie followed the tracks to the edge of the icy creek, where they lost them in the deep snow along the creek bank. A bitter wind rattled the branches of the scrub oak that crowded the creek bank. Jamie hugged her arms across her chest against the cold. "Did they wade across the creek?" she asked. "I don't see any tracks on the other side." Across the creek, the snow covered the open expanse between the creek and the cabins in a smooth white blanket.

"Me, either," Dwight said. "Let's see if we can pick up the tracks somewhere on this side of the creek." He headed one direction, while Jamie started off in the opposite direction. Carefully picking her way around the scrub oak and deadfall, she searched for some sign of the snowshoe tracks they had been following.

After about two minutes, she came upon a place where snow had been cleared away to reveal a stone campfire ring, logs drawn up on three sides for seating. Smoke curled up from the blackened contents of the ring, the scent of wet ash leaving a bitter taste in her mouth. "Dwight!" she called. "I've found something." She leaned over for a closer look and her heart hammered in her throat as she spotted what looked like blond hair.

Crashing sounds heralded Dwight's approach. He jogged up to her. "What is it?" he asked.

She pointed to the fire ring. "The ashes are still hot."

He found a tree branch and used it to poke at the smoldering fire. "There's some cloth in here," he said.

"And what looks like hair," she said. She put a hand to her mouth, fighting a wave of nausea. "You don't think it's a body, do you?"

"It's not real hair, I don't think." He fished a mane of yellow hair, half-melted and streaked black with ash, and held it up. "It's a wig," he said. "A woman's blond wig."

Chapter Fifteen

Nate stood in the situation room at the sheriff's department, trying to ignore the throbbing in his ankle. His doctor probably wouldn't approve of him having ditched the cast boot so soon, but he was sick of hobbling around on it. And he had plenty to distract him from the pain. The evidence collected from the fire pit had been arranged on the table in front of him. In addition to the half-burned blond wig, Jamie and Dwight had retrieved the remains of a wig of black dreadlocks, a fake beard and mustache, and black fabric garments that may have been the pirate costume. Before removing the items, they had photographed and measured the scene, and these photographs were also part of the evidence now.

"Do you think you can get DNA from the wigs?" Nate asked Travis.

"Maybe," the sheriff said. "If they aren't too badly burned. But that doesn't do us any good right now, since we can't get the wigs to the lab to test for DNA."

"I'll get to work adding all of this to our database,"

Jamie said, moving to the computer in the corner of the room.

"Lacy and I are supposed to have dinner with our officiate," Travis said. "But if you need me for anything…"

"You'll be the first to hear if there's a new development," Jamie said.

Travis left and she looked at Nate. "You might as well go home, too."

"I was thinking I could go and get us some dinner," he said.

"I packed a sandwich," she said. "It's in my locker."

"Doesn't something hot from Moe's Pub sound better? My treat." It wasn't the most romantic date he could think of, but it would give them a little time alone to talk.

"All right," she relented. "I guess I could go for a burger."

"No cheese, no onions, right?"

She smiled. "You remember."

"Some things you don't forget." And some people. Even in the years they had been apart, he hadn't forgotten about her. For a long time, she had been his fondest memory from his past. Returning to Eagle Mountain had made him wonder if they could make new memories together in the future.

Go slow, he reminded himself as he headed for his truck. Jamie had made it clear she wouldn't be rushed.

When he returned with their food half an hour later, she was bent over the computer. She looked up when he deposited the brown paper bag containing their burgers on the desk beside her. "Good timing," she said. "I was just finishing up."

He pulled a chair up across from her and handed her the diet soda he knew she preferred, then began distributing the food. "Thanks," she said, unwrapping her burger. "I really am starved."

"Tromping around in the woods in the cold burns a lot of calories," he said.

She nodded as she chewed, then swallowed. "How is your ankle?"

"It's there." He sipped his iced tea. "I guess Donna got home okay this morning?"

"Yes. She had a great time. Mrs. O'Keefe is so nice to take her."

"Are things serious between her and Henry?" he asked. "I mean, are they in love?"

Jamie frowned. "I don't know. They really like each other, but it's hard to say. I mean, Donna loves a lot of things. She loves her favorite TV shows and her stuffed cat and our three dogs. And she loves me. If I asked her, she would probably say she loves Henry, but I'm not sure if she knows what romantic love means."

"We all talk about loving lots of different things," he said. "Donna might not have the vocabulary to describe how her feelings for those things are different, but I'll bet down inside she knows the difference. I think that's part of being human." She stared at him a long moment, until he began to feel uncomfortable. "Did I say something wrong?" he asked.

"No. I think you said something very wise. I have

to remind myself sometimes that my sister is her own person. I'm so used to looking after her and making decisions for her that I forget that sometimes. Her feelings and thoughts are real and valid even if I don't understand them. She's growing and changing all the time, though I don't always remember that."

"What does she do while you're working late like this?" he asked.

"She stays with our neighbor, Mrs. Simmons. She's a retired nurse and she and Donna really get along great. I was lucky to find her."

"I don't imagine that's cheap."

"No. But Donna gets some disability income that helps pay for it, and it's not like I spend my money on much else."

She said this as a kind of a joke, but he knew it was true. Jamie had never been one for fancy clothes or expensive hobbies and as far as he could tell, that hadn't changed. He had dated women who spent more on clothes and shoes and hair care, or cars and theatre tickets and furniture, than Jamie probably made in a year. It wasn't that she didn't care about her appearance or her surroundings, but she considered other things more important. She had dealt with more challenges than most women her age and had had to grow up much faster.

She finished her burger and stuffed the wrapper in the bag, then glanced up at the wall clock. "I should call Donna and tell her goodnight," she said. "I try to do that whenever I'm working late."

While she made the call, he stood and wandered

over to the evidence table. The items they had pulled from the fire ring still reeked of smoke, along with the burnt-plastic smell of the singed artificial hair from the wigs. He picked up the evidence bag that contained the blond wig and examined it more closely.

Jamie joined him at the table. "Where in Eagle Mountain would someone get a wig like this?" he asked.

"The volunteers at the Humane Society thrift store put together a bunch of costumes for the masquerade ball," Jamie said. "When they open Monday morning I thought I'd go over there and ask if they had a blond wig, and if they remember who they sold it to. And the pirate costume. There couldn't have been too many like that, so I'm hoping they'll remember selling it."

Nate laid the wig back on the table. "I don't think it was an accident that they left this stuff near those cabins," he said.

"I don't, either," she said. "They guessed we would look for them there, because they had used that other cabin."

"They're taunting us," Nate said.

"Yes. They've done it before. They killed Fiona Winslow at the scavenger hunt, when there were off-duty officers all around them. They got a charge out of getting away with murder right under our noses."

"That's why the pirate focused on you at the party last night," Nate said. "It's why he drove by your house, and why he was hanging out at the vet's office this afternoon. Your spotting him wasn't an accident. He wanted you to see him and to know he's keeping tabs on you."

She shrugged. "It's creepy, but he's not going to do anything to me. I'm not going to let him trick me into coming with him somewhere. And I'm not going to mistake either Alex or Tim for innocent college students who need a lift somewhere, or a woman who needs help. I know better."

"You need to be careful," he said. "And you shouldn't go out alone."

"I'm alone in my patrol cruiser every time I work a shift," she said. "I know how to handle myself."

"There are two of them and only one of you," Nate said. "Maybe you should partner with another officer until this is over. Talk to Travis."

"No!" Her eyes flashed with anger. "You wouldn't suggest something like that to a male deputy."

"These two aren't killing men," he said.

"And they aren't going to kill me." She sat in front of the computer once more. "I appreciate your concern, but I can look after myself. I've been doing it a long time."

"I know." He shoved his hands in his pockets and stared at the floor, trying to rein in his emotions. "But that doesn't stop me from worrying."

"Nate." Her voice held a note of warning.

"What?"

"If we're going to be a…a couple, then you can't do this."

"I can't worry about you? I don't know how to

stop it. Or is it that you don't want me to talk about being worried?"

"You can worry—just don't try to stop me from doing my job."

If the shoe was on the other foot—if she objected to him going to work every day because it was dangerous—he would hate it. And they would probably fight about it. He wasn't going to let that happen. "I don't want you to give up your job," he said. "And I was out of line, suggesting you partner up with another deputy. I shouldn't have said that."

"Apology accepted." She hesitated, then added. "And it's nice to know someone is concerned about me. It means a lot."

He nodded. What he really wanted was to pull her to him and kiss her, but now wasn't the time or place. "I'd better go," he said. "You've got work to do and I should probably put this ankle up and slap an ice pack on it or something."

"You do that," she said. "I'll see you tomorrow."

He left, leaning more heavily on his cane as he crossed the parking lot to his truck. A thin sliver of moon shone overhead, amidst about a million diamond-bright stars. With few streetlights and most of the businesses shut down for the evening, there was little to compete with the nightly show in the heavens.

Nate drove slowly down Main, past silent storefronts and empty curbs. Moe's Pub, with its single lit sign, was the only business open, and only half a dozen cars and trucks remained in the gravel lot next to the tavern. A man emerged from Moe's front door and waved as Nate drove past, and Nate lifted one finger in salute. When Nate was a teenager, he had hated how quiet things were here after six or seven o'clock. The nearest movie theatre was an hour away and there had been nothing to do and nowhere to hang out with friends, away from the scrutiny of parents and teachers.

Now that he was older, he appreciated the peace and quiet. After a couple of years of partying in college he had had his fill, and these days he would rather watch a movie from the comfort of his couch, or visit with friends in their homes. He chuckled. Was this a sign of maturity—that he had no desire to hang out all night?

He approached the turnoff toward his house but instead of taking it, he drove half a mile farther and made the turn onto Jamie's street. He would just cruise by and make sure everything was all right. Just to help him sleep easier.

He slowed as he neared her house, and tightened his hands on the steering wheel as he took in the dark shape of an SUV in her driveway. Jamie's SUV was parked at the sheriff's department. So who was this? He flicked on his brights, trying to make out the figure in the driver's seat.

Just then, the vehicle in Jamie's driveway roared to life. The SUV reversed out of the driveway and barreled straight at Nate, who only had time to brace himself for the crash.

Chapter Sixteen

"Officer, please respond to MVA, Oak Street."

Jamie keyed her mike and responded. "Unit five responding."

"Copy that, unit five. EMS and fire are also on the way."

Jamie switched on her lights and siren and punched the accelerator. Oak was her street, with little traffic during daylight. Had one of her neighbors come home after too much to drink and clipped another car? Or had the deer who liked to wander into town and eat people's landscaping leaped out in front of a motorist?

As she turned onto the street, her headlights illuminated a pickup truck in front of the house. With a start, she realized it was Nate's truck. He stood beside it, head in his hands. She braked to a stop and, leaving the cruiser running, jumped out of the car and raced to his side. "Nate, what happened?" she asked. "Are you all right?"

"I'm fine. But my truck…" He pointed to the front of the truck. Jamie took a few steps forward and stared at the pile of bricks that had once been her mailbox surround, and at the crushed front end of Nate's pickup, steam hissing from the radiator.

"What happened?" she asked again, but before he could answer, an ambulance approached and parked across the street, followed by a fire truck. Merrily Rayford and Emmett Baxter climbed out of the ambulance and headed for Nate and Jamie, while a trio of firefighters in yellow bunker gear surrounded the truck.

"Is this our victim?" Merrily, a wiry blonde, set down a plastic tote and swept the beam of a flashlight over Nate's face. "That's quite a knot you have there. Did you hit your head on the dash?"

Nate put up a hand to shield his eyes as the EMT spotlighted a golf-ball-sized knot near his right temple. "It was a pretty hard impact. The air bags exploded and I couldn't really see anything for a few seconds." He brushed at the front of his jacket, which was coated in fine white dust. "What a mess."

"Lower your hand so I can see your eyes, please." He did as instructed and Merrily finished her examination. "Are you experiencing any pain?" she asked. "Neck, back, ribs, chest?"

"Just my head."

Merrily flicked a glance at Jamie. "How much did you have to drink tonight?" she asked.

"Nothing," Nate said.

"He hasn't been drinking," Jamie affirmed. "He and I were working at the sheriff's department until twenty minutes ago."

"Then how did you end up taking out this mail-box?" Emmett asked.

"Another vehicle ran me off the road," he said.

Merrily nodded and pressed a gauze square to the knot on Nate's head, which was seeping a little blood. "I don't see any sign of a concussion," she said. "But you ought to have someone with you tonight. And you could have whiplash or other injuries. Sometimes the shock of the accident masks pain. If you start experiencing any other symptoms, you should see a doctor right away."

"All right," he said. "Thanks."

While Merrily and Emmett packed up their gear and returned to the ambulance, Jamie pulled Nate aside. "Who forced you off the road?" she asked.

"That dark gray SUV that's been following you around was parked in your driveway," he said. "I slowed down to get a better look and hit my brights. The vehicle came barreling out the drive and headed right toward me. I had to wrench the wheel over to avoid being hit head-on." He frowned at the pile of crumbled brick in front of his bumper. "Sorry about your mailbox."

"Who was it?" she asked. "Did you get a good look at the driver?"

"No. Whoever it was had a knit cap pulled down low over his forehead, and a scarf wrapped around the lower half of his face."

She stared, trying to take in all he had said. "Are you sure it was the same SUV?" she asked.

"Yes. A Toyota Highlander. He was parked in your

driveway, lights out." She could feel his eyes on her, and she could feel the anger and concern radiating from him, though it was too dark for her to read his expression. "He was waiting for you."

She gripped his arm, as much to steady herself as to command his attention. "What were you doing here?"

He hesitated, then said, "I was headed home and decided to drive by, just to check on the place. I'm not sure why—maybe I had an idea he would try something like this. I don't think it was a coincidence that he drove by here last night, and that he was waiting when you came out of the vet's office this afternoon."

Jamie didn't want to believe that this killer had targeted her. But she had been trained to draw conclusions based on evidence, and the evidence—as well as intuition—told her Nate was right.

"Jamie!"

She turned at the sound of her name. Donna, her puffy purple coat pulled on over pink flannel pajamas, jogged across the lawn toward her. Mrs. Simmons, swathed in a drab car coat, followed at a more sedate pace. "Jamie, what is going on?" Donna asked, throwing her arms around her sister.

"It's okay," Jamie said, hugging Donna to her. Feeling her sister's bulk calmed her. Donna was safe. Nate was going to be all right. That was all that mattered right now. "Just a little accident."

Donna turned to look at Nate. "Nate, are you hurt?" she asked.

His smile was more of a grimace, but Jamie was

touched by the effort. "Just a bump on the head," he said. "I'll be fine."

"Your poor truck!" Donna pointed at the crumpled vehicle. "And the mailbox. How will we get the mail?"

"We can get a new mailbox," Jamie said.

"Such a commotion." Huffing a little, Mrs. Simmons joined them. "We heard the sirens and saw the lights and Donna insisted on coming out to see," she said. Her eyes shone and she kept darting glances at Nate and the wrecked truck, and the firefighters, who had retreated to the fire engine. Jamie suspected the caregiver had been as eager as Donna to be a part of the excitement.

"Did you see what happened?" Jamie asked.

Mrs. Simmons shook her head. "We were watching TV in the back of the house."

"We were watching Bollywood," Donna said. "And I had it turned up loud. I love the music and the dancing."

"But then we heard sirens and I looked out and saw the flashing lights," Mrs. Simmons said. She leaned in closer and lowered her voice to a whisper. "Was it drunk driving, do you think?"

"No," Jamie said. "What about earlier? Did you see anyone over here at my house—another car in the driveway?"

"No." Mrs. Simmons's eyes widened and she put a hand to her mouth. "Someone was at your house? Who?"

"I don't know." Jamie didn't want to frighten the

older woman. "It was probably someone with the wrong address. They weren't looking where they were going when they backed out of the driveway and hit Nate who had to swerve to avoid them."

She jumped as the fire truck's siren bleated. The firefighters waved as they pulled away from the curb. Merrily and Emmett jogged toward the ambulance. "Another call just came in," Emmett said.

The street seemed eerily silent after the emergency vehicles had left them. Jamie's feet and fingers ached with cold. "You need to get inside before you freeze," she told Donna.

"When will you be home?" Donna asked.

"When my shift is over." Jamie patted Donna's shoulder. "You go on back with Mrs. Simmons and I'll see you after eleven." She hoped it wouldn't be much later than that.

"Are you sure everything is all right?" Mrs. Simmons asked.

"It will be fine." She smiled in a way that she hoped was reassuring.

Donna and Mrs. Simmons returned to the caregiver's house and Jamie took out her phone. "I'm going to take some photographs and then I'll call a wrecker for your car."

"I'll get the wrecker driver to take me home," Nate said. "I guess there's nothing else I can do tonight."

"You heard Merrily," Jamie said. "You shouldn't be alone tonight."

"It's just a bump on the head," he said. "I'll be fine." She dug her house keys from her pocket and pressed them into his hands. "You can stay with me tonight. I'll make up the couch." She wasn't ready to deal with awkward questions from Donna just yet.

He looked at the keys. "Are you sure?"

"I'm sure. Make yourself at home. I'll see to your truck, file my report, then I'll pick up Donna and be home before midnight."

She started to turn away, but he touched her arm. "You know what this means, him parked in your driveway?" he asked. "He's decided to go after you."

Her stomach knotted, but she refused to acknowledge the truth of his words. "He may be going after me," she said. "But you're the one who keeps getting hurt."

"I'm tough," he said. "I can take it."

"You don't think I can?"

"You're the strongest woman I know," he said. "But I don't want to have to find out what it would be like to not have you around."

He turned and strode toward the house, with only a trace of a limp. Jamie's chest hurt as she watched him mount the steps to the porch and let himself inside her house, but she didn't know whether the fear that threatened to strangle her was because someone might be trying to kill her—or because Nate cared so much.

NATE WOKE TO a throbbing head, in a room where the light didn't feel quite right. As sleep fled and his vision cleared, he looked up at the woman leaning over him. Donna, a pink knit hat pulled down over her brown hair, a fuzzy pink robe over pink pajamas, looked at him with an expression of great concern. "Hello," she said. "Why are you sleeping on our couch?"

After confirming that he was still dressed, Nate threw off the quilt he'd been sleeping under and shoved into a sitting position. "Jamie thought it would be better if I stayed here instead of going home alone after I was hurt last night," he said.

Donna nodded. "Good idea. Do you want some breakfast? We have cereal, or toaster waffles."

"What kind of cereal?" Nate asked.

Donna scrunched up her nose. "The healthy kind."

He suppressed a laugh. "Then maybe waffles?"

"Good choice!" She whirled and skipped away.

Nate made his way to the bathroom, where he rinsed his mouth and washed his face, and grimaced at the haggard, bruised visage that stared back at him. He ran a hand over his chin, the sandpaper rasp of a day's growth of beard making him wince. Nothing he could do about that now.

The smell of coffee drew him to the kitchen, where Jamie stood before the toaster, an empty plate in one hand, a coffee mug in the other. "Nate's here," Donna announced, unnecessarily, as Jamie had already turned to greet him.

"How are you feeling?" she asked, as he took a mug from the cabinet and filled it from the coffee maker beside the sink.

"I've got a headache, but nothing two aspirin and a little caffeine won't cure." He sipped the coffee and closed his eyes, savoring the sensation of its warmth spreading through him.

"Waffles will make you feel better," Donna said.

"Sit down and I'll fix you some waffles," Jamie said.

"I can look after myself," he said.

"It's not like I'm slaving over a hot stove." She set aside her coffee and pushed him toward the table. The toaster dinged and she plucked two waffles from the slots, dropped them on the plate, then set the plate in front of him. Donna pushed the syrup toward him.

He started to protest that he hadn't meant to take her waffles, but she had already inserted two more frozen discs into the toaster and pulled another plate from the cabinet. Three minutes later, she sat across from him. "I have to take Donna to work at eight, so I can give you a ride to your place," she said.

"Drop me off at the station," he said. "I want to talk to Travis about what happened last night."

"All right." She turned to Donna. "When you get off work this afternoon, wait for Mrs. Simmons to pick you up," she said. "I don't want you walking by yourself today."

"I can walk." Donna mopped up syrup with a forkful of waffle. "I like to walk."

"I know you do, but it's safer right now for you to wait for Mrs. Simmons."

Nate waited for Donna to protest, or to ask why, but she only mumbled "All right," and remained focused on finishing her breakfast. Was she as aware as they were of the danger the Ice Cold Killers posed to a young woman walking by herself? Or had experience taught her she wouldn't win an argument with her sister?

"Remember to wait for Mrs. Simmons," Jamie said. "Don't leave the store on your own."

"I'd rather go home with Henry." Donna looked up from her plate. "His mom said I could come over any time."

"We don't want to take advantage of Mrs. O'Keefe's hospitality," Jamie said. "Besides, if you go over to Henry's house all the time, he might get tired of you."

"He won't get tired of me," she said. "He loves me."

The expression in Jamie's eyes softened, though her mouth was still tight with worry. Nate wondered if he would ever tire of watching her this way—he was beginning to think not.

"Henry asked me to a birthday party tomorrow night," she said. "His cousin's birthday. She lives in a big house and has a hot tub and a snowmobile. She's going to have music and cake, and at midnight, they're going to shoot off fireworks."

"How long have you known about this?" Jamie asked.

Donna stuck out her lower lip. "I forgot to tell you. But Henry's mom is supposed to call you."

"I really don't want you out so late," Jamie said. "Especially with people I don't know. Maybe some other time."

"But I want to go!" Donna stood, her chair skidding backward. "You can't tell me what to do all the time. I'm old enough to decide for myself." Tears streamed down her face as she stared at Jamie. "I want to decide for myself," she sobbed, then whirled and ran from the room.

Jamie stared after her, then laid down her fork and pushed back her chair. She started to rise, then sank back down and turned to Nate. "Do you think I'm wrong?" she asked. "I'm only trying to protect her."

Nate clamped his mouth shut. Getting involved in a dispute between two sisters sounded like a bad idea any time. "You know your sister better than I do," he said.

"She wants to be independent," Jamie said. "She wants to be like other young women her age and it hurts her that she isn't. She doesn't show it, but I know it hurts. It's so unfair—she never did anything to deserve this."

"Neither did you," he said.

The look she gave him was so full of anguish he ached for her. "I want her to be happy," she said. "But most of all, I want her to be safe. Especially now. Especially with this killer preying on local women." She leaned across the table and took his hand. "What do you think I should do? Please tell me."

He took a sip of coffee, buying time. "Why not wait and talk to Mrs. O'Keefe?" he said. "Find out more about this party—where it is and who else will be there. Then you'll have a better idea of the risk involved."

She nodded. "All right. That makes sense." She sat back and let out a breath. "Thanks."

She stood and began gathering dishes. He rose and helped. They worked silently. She filled the dishwasher, while he put away the waffles and syrup—as he had done after other meals he had eaten here when they were in high school.

She had just closed the dishwasher when the doorbell rang. The dogs erupted into barking, a mad scrabble of toenails on the wood floor as they raced for the door. "Company!" Donna called, stomping down the stairs.

By the time Nate and Jamie reached the foyer, Donna was peering out the side window. "It's the sheriff," she announced.

Jamie shushed the dogs and ordered them back, then opened the door for Travis. He had his back to them, surveying the ruined mailbox. When he turned around, he didn't seem surprised to see Nate standing with Jamie. "I heard about what happened here last night," he said. "Jamie's report said something about a dark gray Highlander?"

"Come in." Jamie stepped back and held the door open wider. "Donna, you'd better go upstairs and get dressed or you'll be late."

Nate braced himself for another protest, but Donna merely turned and headed upstairs again. "Would you like some coffee?" Jamie asked. "I can make a fresh pot."

"No, thanks." He turned to Nate. "Tell me what happened."

Nate repeated his story about seeing the SUV in Jamie's driveway and gave his description of the driver.

"To anyone passing, he'd look like someone bundled up against the cold," Travis said. "But he made sure you wouldn't be able to give a description of him."

"I'm sure it's Alex or Tim," Nate said. "Everything points to it. I'd recognize the vehicle again. If we can find it, maybe we can find them."

"That's another reason I stopped by this morning," Travis said. "We found the Highlander. The VIN matches the one owned by Tim Dawson."

"That's great," Jamie said. "If they've been using it all this time, there's bound to be evidence—hairs, fibers, DNA."

Travis didn't seem nearly as excited as Jamie about the find. Then again, the sheriff was not the most emotional person around. "Where did you find it?" Nate asked.

"Out on Forest Service Road 1410, near the Sundance cabins," Travis said. "A call came in about eleven last night that someone had seen a fire in that area. By the time the first pumper truck got there, it was burned down to the frame."

"Accident or arson?" Nate asked.

"Oh, it was deliberate," Travis said. "The fire crew said they could smell the diesel fuel before they even got out of their truck."

"They were destroying evidence," Jamie said.

"Yes," Travis said. "And destroying our best link to them."

Chapter Seventeen

"Some folks nicknamed it the green monster." Bud O'Brien slapped his gloved hand on the hood of a mostly-green vintage pickup truck with oversize tires. "It looks like crap, but it will get you where you want to go."

"I guess I don't have much choice," Nate said, accepting the keys from the garage owner. His own truck was awaiting an assessment by an insurance appraiser—something that wouldn't happen until the highway reopened. Estimates on when that would be varied from tomorrow to next week, or next month. It all depended on how fast a road crew could clear away the many avalanches that had covered the pavement and how long fresh snows held off.

Today was sunny, the glittering white of the landscape blinding, the sky the blue of lake ice, the air bitterly cold and sharp enough that a deep breath was painful. The green monster's tires crunched over the snow-packed road as Nate headed out of town. Though he had discarded the air boot on his ankle and managed to walk without limping at least half the time, he hadn't been cleared to return to work, and Travis had nothing new for him to do. He'd decided to check out the site where Alex and Tim had burned their truck, more out of curiosity than from any hope of finding a real clue.

Bud O'Brien had hauled away what was left of the vehicle that morning, but a blackened patch of earth and soot-stained snow marked the spot, at the entrance to the summer cabins. Nate parked his truck well past the site and walked back along the road, then circled the patch of melted snow and ash that formed a muddy slurry. The smell of burned rubber and diesel fuel lingered in the air, and bits of broken glass and melted rubber littered the area. The deep tracks of Bud's wrecker led from the site to the road.

Nate's examination offered no new insight, so he walked back up toward the cabins, retracing the path he'd taken the day he was injured, wondering if any evidence lay buried under the thick snow, and trying to piece together the events of the last twelve hours. Alex and Tim must have driven out here last night immediately after one of them tried to run him down. The other would have followed in whatever vehicle they were using now—a stolen car? Travis would have zeroed in on any recently stolen vehicles, but he hadn't mentioned anything in the briefing at the sheriff's department that morning.

He had almost reached the cabin where he had been injured when movement in the underbrush caught his attention. At first he thought he had startled a deer, but a flash of red and blue made him reject that notion. Someone—no, two people—were running away from the cabin.

He started after then, but the deep snow and his still-tender ankle brought him to a quick halt. He'd never catch those two this way. He held his breath and listened as his quarry moved away, thrashing and cursing marking their progress. They were headed toward the road that ran behind the cabins, but thick brush and snow impeded their progress. If Nate hurried, he might be able to head them off.

Ignoring the pain in his ankle, he took off running again, this time along the road, the snow there still packed down from sheriff's department vehicles, making movement easier. When he reached his truck, he gunned the engine. For all its dilapidated appearance, the vehicle had plenty of power. He raced around the hairpin curve where the road wound behind the cabins. He spotted the truck, and two figures emerging from the woods and climbing the snow-covered embankment toward a dirty brown Jeep Wrangler.

Nate braked hard and angled the truck in front of the Jeep. They wouldn't be able to move forward without hitting him, and backing up would send them perilously close to the embankment. As the two suspects reached the Jeep, Nate emerged from his truck, his Glock drawn. "Stop, and put your hands up where I can see them," he ordered.

The two young men—teenagers, he guessed—inched their hands into the air. This wasn't Alex and Tim. So why had they run from him? "Don't shoot," the slighter of the two said, staring out from beneath a red knit beanie and a fringe of blond bangs with frightened blue eyes.

"Who are you?" His companion, a handsome, broad-shouldered kid dressed all in black, demanded.

"Officer Nate Hall," he said. "Who are you?"

The teens looked at each other. "We haven't done anything wrong," the blond said.

"You were trespassing on private property," Nate said. Technically, the land on which the cabins sat belonged to the Forest Service, but the cabins themselves were private. "What were you doing at the cabins?"

"We were just looking for a friend," the blond said. His voice wavered and his hands shook.

"Who were you looking for?"

"We don't know their names," the boy dressed darker said. His expression wasn't exactly a sneer, but he showed none of his friend's nervousness. "They're just a couple of climbers we met. We followed them here and figured they were staying at the cabins."

"When did you meet them?" Nate asked.

The darker boy shrugged. "I don't know. A week ago?"

"It was last Monday," his friend said.

"Turn around and place your hands against the vehicle." Nate motioned with the Glock.

"You don't have any right—" the dark-haired boy said.

"He's got a gun," the other boy said. "Just do what he says."

Nate frisked each of them. They weren't armed, but he extracted their wallets and flipped them open. "Giuseppe Calendri and Greg Eicklebaum," he said, examining the driver's license photos, which gave local addresses. He holstered the Glock and returned the wallets, then took out the flyer with the pictures of Alex and Tim and held it out to them. "Are these the two climbers you met?" he asked.

The darker boy—Giuseppe—stuck out his lower lip. "I don't know."

"They had on stocking caps and sunglasses," the blond, Greg, said. "These look like driver's license photos. Nobody really looks like their driver's license photo, do they?"

Nate folded the flyer and stuck it back in his pocket. "Why did you run from me just now?" he asked.

"We didn't know you were a cop," Greg said. "You could have been anybody. I mean, there's a guy running around killing people. For all we knew, that was you."

"The Ice Cold Killer only kills women," Nate said.

"So far," Greg said. "But what if he changes his mind?"

"And it's not like you're in uniform, or even in a cop car." Giuseppe frowned. "You didn't show us a badge, either."

Nate pulled out his ID and flipped it open.

The boys leaned over to study it. "Aww, man," Greg said. "You're not even a real cop."

"I'm a real cop." Nate returned his credentials to his pocket.

"Well, we aren't fishing without a license or hunting out of season," Giuseppe said, his cockiness back. "And we didn't do anything to those cabins. Maybe we just got lost while we were out hiking and decided to cut through there to our car."

Nate didn't waste time arguing with him. "You can go," he said. "For now."

He waited until the boys were in their vehicle before he got into his own and pulled up far enough to let them out. Then he fell in behind them and followed them all the way to town. They turned off toward the gated neighborhood where they both lived, and Nate headed to the sheriff's department, to find out more about Giuseppe Calendri and Greg Eicklebaum.

Jamie and Travis were going over the evidence database she had compiled when Nate walked into the office. How long was it going to be before this goofy, lightheaded feeling stopped sweeping over her every time she saw him? She had to fight to keep a sappy smile from her face, though there was no way she couldn't look at him. If nothing else, she wanted to see if she could detect whatever Donna had seen that convinced her sister that Nate was in love with her.

Okay, so maybe there was a little extra warmth in his eyes. And he really looked at her, his gaze lingering, instead of just sweeping over her. But that didn't really mean he was in love—did it?

"What can you tell me about Giuseppe Calendri and Greg Eicklebaum?" Nate asked, sinking into the chair Travis offered him.

"Where did you run into those two?" Travis asked.

"At Sundance cabins," Nate said. "I wanted to see where Alex and Tim burned the Highlander, then I walked up to the cabins. Those two took off through the woods like a couple of startled deer."

"Giuseppe goes by Pi," Travis said. "He and Greg and a third boy, Gus Elcott, got in a little trouble a couple of weeks ago. They had some kind of competition going, racking up points for whoever could do the most outrageous dare. I had them do community service, shoveling snow, as punishment."

"I think they know something about Alex and Tim," Nate said. "When I asked them what they were doing at the cabins, they said they met a couple of climbers last Monday. They thought they were staying at the cabins and were looking for them. I showed them the pictures of Alex and Tim and they said they didn't recognize them, but I think they're lying."

"Do you know Pi and Greg?" Travis asked Jamie.

She shook her head. "I remember seeing their names as possible witnesses for Christy O'Brien's murder."

"They were spotted near the site of the murder that night," Travis said. "But they swore they didn't see a thing." He stood. "I think you and I should have a talk with Pi. He's the ringleader of that group."

"He struck me as a smug brat," Nate said.

"He's smart," Travis said. "He'll make a good witness if we can get him to tell us what he knows."

"Why did you want to take me to question this boy, instead of Nate?" Jamie asked when she and Travis were in the sheriff's cruiser, headed toward the exclusive neighborhood where the Calendris lived.

"I could say I want to give you more experience questioning suspects," Travis said. "That's true, and it would be the politically correct answer. But also, Nate already struck out questioning the boys. He cornered them and they dug in their heels. Pi strikes me as the type who likes to be the star of the show. You're closer to his age, and a woman, so I think he'll want to impress you."

Jamie smiled. She could always count on the sheriff to be honest. "I'll do my best to appear to hang on his every word," she said.

Chapter Eighteen

The Calendris lived in an impressive stone-and-cedar home with views of the snow-capped mountains. The young man who answered Travis's knock was handsome as any teen heartthrob, with thick dark hair flopping over his brow and deep-set, intense brown eyes. "Hello, Sheriff," he said, showing no surprise at the lawman's appearance. He nodded to Jamie as she walked past. "Hello, Deputy."

He closed the door and led them into an expansive great room, with soaring fir-plank ceilings and a massive stone fireplace in which a fire crackled. "I suppose you're here to ask me more about the two climbers we told Officer Hall about," he said, taking a seat on an oversize leather ottoman. "I'm sorry, I really don't know anything else to tell you."

"Where did you meet them?" Travis asked.

"Those ice falls by the national forest campground," Pi said. "It's not an official climbing area, but with all the snow and cold we've had this winter, there are some impressive features there. We wanted to give it a try and they were just finishing up a climb, but they gave us some good route-finding tips."

"Who is we?" Travis asked.

"Gus Elcott and Greg Eicklebaum were with me." Pi flashed a smile at Jamie. "They were busy unloading our climbing gear, so I did most of the talking with the two climbers."

"Did they tell you their names?" Jamie asked.

Pi shook his head. "No."

"Did they say where they were from? Where they were staying?" Travis asked.

"No."

"You told Officer Hall that you had followed them to the cabins," Travis said. "When was that?"

Pi waved a hand. "Oh, after we finished climbing I thought I spotted the guys' truck on the side of the road. I slowed down, thinking I'd stop and thank them for their help, and ask if they knew other good climbing areas around there. But as I slowed down, they pulled out in front of me. So I followed them until they pulled into the cabins. When they saw me, though, they pulled out and left."

"If they left, what made you think they were staying there?" Jamie asked.

Pi shrugged. "Just a hunch I had. I believe in following hunches."

"Have you seen either of these two since that day?" Travis asked.

"No." He leaned forward, elbows on his knees. "Why are you so interested in them? Have they done something wrong?"

"We'd like to question them in connection with a case," Travis said.

Pi sat back and nodded. "You think they have something to do with those women who were murdered," Pi said. "Maybe they're the Ice Cold Killer. I'm right, aren't I?"

"Describe these two," Travis said, ignoring Pi's suspicions. "How old do you think they were? What did they look like?"

"They were in their twenties, I think," Pi said. "One was about my height—six feet—and the other was an inch or two taller."

"What color hair?" Travis prompted.

Pi shook his head. "They were wearing knit caps and those face things—balaclavas? It was really cold out, and when you're climbing ice, it gets even colder."

"What color eyes?"

"They had on sunglasses."

"Anything else?" Travis asked. "Did they have accents? Say where they were from?"

"No. We just talked about climbing."

Travis frowned, but closed his notebook and stood. Jamie and Pi rose also. "What are you and Greg and Gus up to these days, besides climbing?" Travis asked.

"We're staying out of trouble," Pi said.

"No more dares?"

Pi laughed. "No more dares. Thought it was fun while it lasted. Gus ended up with the most points, though we never declared an official winner."

"Points?" Jamie asked.

Pi flashed his movie-star smile again—a smile that had probably left more than one teenage girl weak at the knees, Jamie thought. "We had a little competition going where we accumulated points for different accomplishments. Some of them were a little risky, but we didn't mean any harm." He glanced at Travis. "Though I guess things were getting a little out of hand there at the end. It was probably just as well that we stopped."

"Don't start up again," Travis said. "Someone might get hurt."

"We won't," Pi said as he walked them to the door. "Although I think about it sometimes, things I might have done to earn more points. Just as a mental exercise, of course." He opened the door and Travis and Jamie exited. Pi followed them onto the steps. "I hope you catch your killers," he said. "That's something that would have been worth a lot of points when we were playing our game. Someone who caught a serial killer would have been the ultimate winner."

"This isn't a game," Travis said. "If you know something that would help us, you need to tell us."

"I don't know anything," Pi said, his expression remaining pleasant. "Just another mental exercise." He returned to the house and closed the door behind him.

"There's something he's not telling us," Jamie said as she buckled her seat belt. "We need to talk to Greg and see what he says."

"We'll talk to Greg." Travis started the cruiser.

"And maybe Pi is hiding something. Or maybe he just wants us to think he's smarter than he is."

"He probably isn't smarter than the killers," Jamie said.

"They're making mistakes," Travis said. "Leaving behind more evidence. We're going to find them."

"That would be a nice wedding present, wouldn't it?" Jamie said. "Closing this case before you leave on your honeymoon."

"Yeah," Travis agreed. "I know Lacy would appreciate it if we could start our marriage without this hanging over us."

"They haven't killed anyone in six days," Jamie said. "Maybe because we're closing in on them, forcing them to spend more time running."

"I wish I could think that's a good thing," he said. "But everything I've read says serial killers feel compelled to chase the high they get from killing. It's like a drug and the longer they go without it, the more the craving builds."

She bit the inside of her cheek, trying to create some saliva for her suddenly dry mouth. "Nate thinks the killers have targeted me," she said.

"I don't think he's wrong," Travis said. He glanced at her, then refocused his attention on the road. "That's another reason I wanted you with me this afternoon. I don't want you patrolling alone until this is settled. And before you say anything, I would do the same if a killer appeared to be stalking a male deputy."

"Yes, sir." As much as she wanted to protest that her training enabled her to look after herself, the truth was, these two killers frightened her. She never wanted to be in the position where she had to face them down alone.

MONDAY AFTERNOON, JAMIE devoted herself to helping Donna get ready for the party. Henry's mom had answered all her questions and reassured her that the birthday party would be well supervised and safe. Donna could enjoy the party and Jamie didn't have to feel like a terrible person for keeping her home. Donna had been ecstatic at the news and had spent hours going through her clothes, deciding what to wear

Though her sister had attended homecoming dances and senior prom with groups of friends, and she had met Henry and his mother at the masquerade ball, this was her first real date, and she threw herself into it with all the fanfare of a Hollywood actress preparing for her first red carpet premiere. A long bubble bath was followed by a session with blow dryer and curling iron. She sat in a kitchen chair before her dresser mirror and fidgeted while Jamie shaped her hair into dozens of short ringlets all over her head.

"Close your eyes," Jamie ordered before she sprayed a liberal application of hair spray. A sparkly pink bow carefully clipped over one ear formed the finishing touch. Though Jamie had feared the final effect would be more French poodle than *femme fatale*, Donna ended up looking perfectly lovely.

"I need perfume," Donna said, jumping up from her chair. "Something that smells really good."

Jamie didn't normally wear perfume, but she unearthed a bottle of her mother's favorite scent in the back of a closet. She dabbed some on Donna's wrist and her sister sniffed appreciatively. "It smells pretty," she said. "Like Mom, when she dressed up to go out."

Jamie had a sudden memory of watching her mother put on her makeup before going out to dinner with their father. When she was done, she would call both girls to her and give them a little spritz of her perfume "to have a little bit of me with you while I'm away." Now it felt like she was here again with them. "Mama would be so proud of you now," Jamie said, then turned away before she started crying and Donna, always so sympathetic to others' emotions, joined in. "Let's finish getting you ready."

Half an hour before Henry and his mother were due to arrive, Donna stood before Jamie. The orange ribbed tights she had chosen to go with her pink party dress—because orange was Henry's favorite color—made her look like a sherbet dessert—but a charming one. Henry would no doubt be delighted. Jamie's gaze shifted to the silver high heels Donna had borrowed from Jamie's closet. "Are you sure you don't want your pink flats?" she asked. "They'll be more comfortable for dancing."

"I don't want to be comfortable," Donna said. "I want to be pretty."

"Your flats are very pretty," Jamie said, resisting the impulse to rant about a culture that made women believe beauty was something they had to suffer for. Donna didn't care about any of that—she just wanted to be like the other young women she saw, with their high heels and fancy dresses.

"Is my face okay?' Donna turned and peered anxiously into the mirror. With Jamie's help, she wore not only powder and lip gloss, but eye shadow and mascara, which made her look older and, yes, more sophisticated.

"You look beautiful," Jamie said, hugging her gently, so as not to muss her hair.

The doorbell rang and the dogs began to bark. The sisters raced downstairs to answer it, but instead of Henry and his mother, Nate stood on the doorstep, his arms full of flowers. "Hello," he said. He offered a bouquet to Donna. "These are for you."

"Flowers!" Donna buried her nose in the blossoms—a handful of pink and white carnations and a single overblown rose.

"And these are for you." Nate extended a second bouquet—more carnations and alstroemeria—to Jamie.

"Where did you find flowers?" she asked. "I'm sure the florist hasn't had a delivery in weeks."

"They had a few blooms left," he said. He turned back to Donna. "You look beautiful."

She blushed and giggled, and teetered on her heels, so that Jamie reached out to steady her. She should find a way to pull Mrs. O'Keefe aside and give her the pink flats, in case Donna wanted to change later.

"What should I do with my flowers?" Donna asked.

"I'll put them in a vase," Jamie said. She took her sister's bouquet along with her own to the kitchen, glad for a few moments alone to organize her thoughts. Nate's arrival was a surprise, but it didn't feel wrong to have him here for this milestone. She wondered if he understood how important this was for her and for Donna, too, and wanted to celebrate with them. Maybe he did, since he had brought the flowers.

Voices drew her back to the foyer, where Henry stood, dressed in black jeans and boots, a Western-cut white shirt, black leather jacket and a string tie. "Henry, you look so handsome," Donna cooed.

"And you look beautiful," he said, eyes shining.

Donna turned to Jamie. "And look—he brought me a corsage."

Jamie duly admired the corsage—made of pink silk roses and silk ferns—and slid it onto Donna's wrist. "Before you go, I have to get a picture," Jamie said, rushing to retrieve her phone.

The resulting photos showed the couple arm in arm, grinning at the camera, then at each other. Donna had never looked happier, Jamie thought.

"We have to go," Henry said.

Nate helped Donna with her coat. He and Jamie followed the couple onto the front porch and waved to Mrs. O'Keefe, who waited in the car.

Back inside, Jamie stood for a moment with her head down, one knuckle pressed hard above her upper lip, determined to hold back tears. Nate put his arm around her. "I can't believe I'm being so silly," she said. "You'd think I was sending my only kid to war or something. It's just a dance."

"I'm wondering if it's because she's doing something you thought she might never do," Nate said. "She's going on a real date with a young man she loves. She's doing something other girls her age do all the time, but that not every girl with her disability gets to do or is able to do."

Jamie looked up at him, blinking hard and somehow managing to keep the tears from overflowing. "I never thought of that," she said. "I... I think you might be right."

He took her hand in his. "I figured you might appreciate a little distraction tonight, so I thought I'd take you out."

"A real date?" she asked.

"A real date." He surveyed the yoga pants and sweatshirt she wore. "I can wait while you change."

She laughed and punched his chest. Unlike her casual clothes, he wore pressed jeans, a dark blue dress shirt and sports coat. "What makes you think I need to change?"

He grinned and waggled his eyebrows. "I can help you, if you like."

"Then we might never leave the house."

"I'm liking this idea better and better." He lunged toward her and she danced out of his reach and raced up the stairs.

"I'll be down in ten minutes," she called over her shoulder.

A pleasant thrill of excitement hummed through her as she rifled through her closet, trying to choose the right outfit. She settled on a pale blue cashmere sweater, black tights, a short black skirt and tall leather boots. Warm, easy to move in, but still sexy.

She was leaning over the bathroom sink, finishing her makeup, when Nate entered, a glass of wine in each hand. "I thought you might like this." He handed her a glass.

She sipped, her eyes locked to his. Despite the fading black eye and bruised temple, he had never looked more handsome to her. Maturity sat well on him, and though she still recognized the boy he had been, she appreciated more the man he had become.

She set aside the wine glass and wrapped her arms around him. "This was a good idea," she said.

"The wine? Or the date."

"The date."

He set his own glass beside hers, then drew her close for a kiss—not the eager kiss of an impatient lover or the perfunctory embrace of a man doing what was expected, but a deep, tender caress that invited lingering and exploration.

She arched her body to his and angled her mouth to draw even closer, sinking into the sensation of his body wrapped around her and the response of her own. Her pulse thrummed in her ears and all thought of anything or anyone fled, and with it every bit of tension that had lately strained her nerves and disturbed her sleep.

She moaned in protest when Nate pulled away, and opened her eyes to stare at him accusingly. "Your phone," he said, gesturing toward the bedroom.

Then she realized a tinny reproduction of an old-fashioned phone ring was echoing from the bedroom. She pushed past him and retrieved the phone from the dresser. When she saw Mrs. O'Keefe's name her relaxed happiness vanished. "Hello? Mrs. O'Keefe, is everything all right?"

"Oh, Jamie!" Mrs. O'Keefe's voice broke in what sounded like a sob. "I'm so sorry. I don't know what to do."

"What is it? What happened?" Nate moved in behind her and she glanced back at him, sure her eyes reflected her sense of panic, then held the phone a little away from her ear so that he could hear, too.

"I stopped to get gas and went inside to pay," Mrs. O'Keefe said, the words pouring out in a rush. "I was sure Henry and Donna would be fine while I was away, but when I came out, she was gone."

"Gone? Donna is gone?" Jamie's voice rose, on the edge of hysteria. Nate's arm encircled her, holding her up as her knees threatened to buckle. "Where is she?"

"I don't know!" Mrs. O'Keefe wailed. "Henry said two men in masks grabbed her and dragged her from the car. One of them hit him—he's bleeding, and when I got there he was hysterical. A sheriff's deputy is here, but I knew I needed to call you."

"We're on our way." Jamie ended the call and grabbed her keys from the dresser. "We have to go," she said, already running for the stairs. "Someone's taken Donna."

Chapter Nineteen

Nate drove as fast as he dared from Jamie's house to the corner where Eagle Mountain's two gas stations stood opposite each other. It had started to snow again, and the streets were mostly empty. Mrs. O'Keefe's Honda sat beside the end gas pump, a sheriff's department cruiser behind it. Jamie was out of the truck before Nate had come to a complete stop, hurrying to where Gage stood with Mrs. O'Keefe beside her vehicle. When Mrs. O'Keefe saw Jamie approaching, she burst into sobs.

Gage moved to one side while Jamie embraced the older woman. Nate approached him. "What have you got?" Nate asked.

"Two men in a white soft-top Jeep pulled up. One got out, jerked open the back door of the O'Keefe car and slashed the seat belt. He clamped one hand over Donna's mouth and dragged her out of the vehicle. When Henry tried to go after them, he punched him—hard. I think the poor kid's nose is probably broken."

"Did anyone see what happened?"

Gage shook his head. "Mrs. O'Keefe was the only customer and the clerk was busy with her."

Nate nodded toward a camera mounted above the gas pumps. "Maybe we'll get something from that."

"Maybe," Gage said. "But the camera is focused next to the pumps, to catch people who drive off without paying for their gas. The kidnappers pulled up on the far side of the O'Keefe car. Henry says they wore masks."

"We don't need to see them to know who did this," Nate said.

The ambulance pulled in on the other side of the gas pumps, followed by the sheriff's cruiser.

EMT Emmett Baxter climbed out and approached the car. Mrs. O'Keefe and Travis met him. Jamie walked over to stand with Gage and Nate, her arms hugged tightly across her chest. The lighting under the gas pump canopy cast a sickly yellow glow, and snow blew around them in dizzying swirls.

Nate went to his truck and retrieved his coat and put it around her shoulders. "It's freezing out here," he said.

"I don't even feel it," she said. "I don't feel anything." Her eyes met his, red-rimmed and bleak. "What if they kill her?"

"You can't think that," he said.

She glanced over toward the car, where Henry sat in the back seat. "Go see about Henry," she said. "He had to see it happen, and he tried to protect her." She covered her mouth with her hand. He started to reach for her, but she pulled away. "Go make sure Henry is okay."

Henry sat between Emmett and his mother in the back seat of the Honda. Nate opened the passenger door and leaned in. "How's it going?" he asked.

"His nose is broken," Emmett said. "We'll have to splint it." He turned back to Mrs. O'Keefe. "We can give him something for the pain first, if you think that's all right."

"Of course." Mrs. O'Keefe squeezed her son's hand. "It's going to be all right," she said.

"It won't be all right without Donna," he moaned.

"Give me your other hand," Mrs. O'Keefe said. "And look at me."

Henry opened his hand and stared at the crumpled rectangle of white pasteboard in it.

"What have you got there?" Mrs. O'Keefe asked.

Nate leaned in past her. "Let me see," he said.

Henry held out his hand and Nate stared at the crumpled business card. "Ice cold," he read.

"He shoved this into my hand before he took Donna away," Henry said.

Nate took the card carefully, holding it by the edges, and walked over to where Travis stood with Jamie. When she saw what he held, her face blanched white, but she said nothing.

Travis frowned at the card. "This doesn't fit the pattern for the other women," he said.

"No, it doesn't," Nate said. "The others were all alone, taken when no one else was around."

Travis turned to Jamie. "Did you see any strange

cars around your house when the O'Keefes and Donna left there this evening?"

"No." She bit her lip. "But I wasn't really looking."

"I didn't see anyone, either," Nate said. He had been focused on Jamie. Still, if Alex and Tim had been there, wouldn't he have known?

"I think they were watching your house and followed Mrs. O'Keefe to the gas station," Travis said. "They saw their chance to grab Donna and took it."

"But why Donna?" Jamie asked. "She never hurt anyone!"

It was the question everyone left behind when a loved one senselessly died asked—the question the families of Kelly Farrow and Christy O'Brien and Michaela Underwood and all the other murder victims had asked. Usually, there was no explanation for a crime like this.

"I don't think they were really after Donna," Travis said.

"Then why?" Jamie looked dazed.

"I think they were after you," Travis said. "This was a way to get to you. To get to a cop. It's what they've wanted all along."

"They can have me," she said. "As long as they don't hurt Donna."

"They're not going to have either of you," Travis said.

"We have to figure out where they've taken her," Nate said. "They have to be holed up somewhere."

Gage emerged from the gas station office. "The security camera at the pump picked up a partial plate number for the vehicle the kidnappers were in," he said. He handed Travis a slip of paper.

"It's the last two numbers of a Colorado plate," Travis said. "That will help—the first three letters are the same for half the cars registered in the county, but the last three are different." He returned the paper to Gage. "Call this in to Dwight. Tell him to do a search for every white Jeep Wrangler in the county and see if he can match this."

"I'm on it," Gage said.

"Let me help," Jamie said. "I'm good on the computer and focusing on the search will help keep me from going crazy."

Travis looked at her a long moment, as if trying to decide if she was going to crack up. "All right," he said. "Go help Dwight."

"I'll take you," Nate said.

They drove to the station in silence. There was no sense trying to comfort Jamie with words. The only thing that counted was action. He parked in front of the sheriff's department and came around to open the door for her. She slipped off his jacket and pressed it on him. "Are you coming in?" she asked.

He shook his head. "No. I'm going to talk to Pi and Greg again. Neither were very forthcoming when we interviewed them earlier, but Travis thinks they know something they aren't telling us, and I'm going to find out what that is."

But when Mrs. Calendri answered the door and Nate showed her his ID, she told him her son wasn't at home. "He's with Greg and Gus," she said.

"Could you call him for me?" Nate shoved his hands in the pocket of his jacket, which still carried a faint whiff of the lotion Jamie used. "It's important."

She retreated into the house and returned with a phone in her hand. She held it to her ear for a moment, then shook her head. "He isn't answering." Another pause, then she said, "Pi, please call your mother as soon as you can. It's important." She ended the call.

"Do you know Greg and Gus's numbers?" Nate asked.

"No. I don't. What is this about? Is Pi in some kind of trouble?"

"I hope not, Mrs. Calendri. We're trying to find someone who may be involved in a crime, and we think your son might be able to help us."

The lines around her eyes tightened. "I don't have Greg and Gus's numbers, but I can tell you where they live."

Greg Eicklebaum lived only two blocks away. Nate drove there and found him and Gus playing video games in a den off the garage. "We don't know where Pi is," Greg said after Nate explained his mission. "He was supposed to come over this afternoon, then said he had something else to do."

Nate sat and faced the boys, so close to them their knees almost touched. "You've got to tell me everything you know about those two climbers you saw out near the campground that day," he said. "We think they kidnapped a young disabled woman this evening. Her life may depend on us finding them." His throat tightened as he said the words, but he pushed the image of Donna, helpless and afraid, away. He had a job to do, and that meant staying focused on facts, not emotions.

The two boys exchanged glances, then Gus said, "We saw one of them this morning."

"Where?"

"We were walking over to the park to shoot hoops." He gestured to the north. "This white Jeep pulled up to the stop sign and we looked over and it was one of the guys—the taller one, with the lighter hair. I remembered his sunglasses—really sharp Oakleys. We waved, but I don't think he saw us."

"You don't know where he was driving from—or where he went?" Nate asked.

"No," Gus said. "But Pi figured he must live near here, because nobody else really drives around here. I mean, there aren't any through streets or anything."

"Can you think of anything else that could help us find this guy?" Nate asked.

They both shook their heads. "I wish we could," Greg said. "Really."

"If you think of anything, call the sheriff's office," Nate said.

He returned to the sheriff's department and found Gage and the sheriff huddled with Dwight and Jamie in the situation room. "We think we've got something," Gage said when Nate joined them.

"There are a lot of white Jeeps registered in the county," Dwight said, tapping the keys of a laptop open on the desk before him. "But only two with the two numbers the security camera caught. One is registered to Amber Perry of 161 Maple Court, the other to Jonathan Dirkson of 17 Trapper Lane."

"Trapper Lane," Nate said.

The others stared at him. "Trapper Lane is in the same neighborhood as Pi Calendri and Greg Eicklebaum," he said. "I just talked to Greg and Gus Elcott, and Greg said they saw one of the climbers they had run into earlier, driving a white Jeep in their neighborhood this morning."

"What's the contact information for Dirkson?" Travis said.

"I'm on it," Jamie said, furiously typing at a second laptop. "Jonathan Dirkson's contact information is in Phoenix," she said.

"That's it!" Nate said. "The house on Trapper Lane is probably a vacation home. Alex and Tim broke into an unoccupied home and made use of the vehicle that was probably in the garage."

"A lot of houses in that neighborhood are second homes," Gage said. "And a lot of people rent them out short-term. Alex and Tim could tell anyone who asked they were vacationing here and the chances of anyone checking with the house's owner are slim to none."

"Let's go," Travis said.

Jamie shoved back her chair. "I'm coming with you," she said. "And don't tell me to stay here. If I'm really the one they want, then maybe I can help to trap them."

"All right." Travis turned to Nate. "I suppose you're going to come, too."

"You could use another trained officer."

"Go with Jamie, in her cruiser," Travis said. "And try not to get hurt. I don't want to have to explain to your boss how you were injured yet again when you aren't even officially on duty."

FOUR SHERIFF'S DEPARTMENT CRUISERS—and most of the sheriff's department, plus Nate—blockaded both ends of Trapper Lane. They surrounded the house, and the sheriff used a bullhorn to demand that Tim and Alex release Donna and come out with their hands up. But the only reaction they received was silence, and furtive looks through the curtains from the neighbors.

Dwight approached the house from the side, then returned to the others. "The Jeep isn't in the garage," he said. "Maybe they aren't here."

"Then we search the house," Travis said.

While the others hung back to provide cover, he and Gage approached the front door. Travis knocked, then tried the knob, and the door swung open. They disappeared into the house and emerged a long five minutes later. "It's clear," Travis called.

The others entered the empty, though orderly, house. Dust covers draped the furniture in every room but the kitchen and a small den where Tim and Alex had apparently established themselves. A couple of sleeping bags were rolled up on the floor of the den, and a few empty cans in the kitchen garbage can were the only evidence of occupation.

"Search every room," Travis said. "I want anything that might be tied to them, or that might tell us where they are now."

Dwight found Donna's corsage on the floor of the mudroom, the flowers crushed. Jamie stared at the forlorn flowers, then turned away, breathing hard.

"I noticed a shed out back," Dwight said. "Some-one should check that."

"I will," Jamie said. She needed to get out of this house where her sister had been held.

The shed was a prefab wooden structure, about five feet by seven feet, with a single door. The door wasn't locked, but Jamie had to force it open. When she finally stepped inside, she saw the reason for her difficulty as she shone her flashlight over the body of Pi Calendri. Her heart sank as she passed the light over the wound in his shoulder and the pool of blood on the concrete floor.

"Somebody help me," he moaned, and Jamie dropped to her knees beside him.

"Pi, what happened?" she asked, feeling for his pulse.

But she never heard his answer, as her head ex-ploded in pain, and the world went black.

Chapter Twenty

Jamie came to in a fog of pain. Her head pounded and her arms ached, and the smell of dust and old wood smoke mingled with the haunting scent of her mother's perfume. As her head cleared, she realized she was lying on a bed, her hands bound beneath her back. Dusty wood beams stretched overhead and nothing looked familiar. She turned her head to the side and relief surged through when she saw a teary-eyed Donna staring back at her, and the memory of being with Pi in the garden shed returned. Someone must have attacked her and brought her to this place. "Are you all right?" Jamie whispered.

"I tore my tights," Donna said. "And I lost my flowers."

Before they could talk more, the door opened and a young man in a blue beanie and parka shuffled in. "Who are you and what are you doing with us?" Jamie asked.

"You don't know who I am?" He chuckled. "I'm the Ice Cold Killer."

Jamie recognized him now, from the flyer Travis

had printed. Tim Dawson. "There are two of you," Jamie said. "Where's your friend?"

"So you figured that out, did you?" He stripped off his coat to reveal a faded red sweatshirt over jeans, then dropped into a straight-backed wooden chair. "He had some things he had to take care of."

"What are you going to do with us?" she asked.

"What do you think?" He clasped his hands behind his head. "The same thing we did to the others. My friend is out there now, looking for a good place to dump your bodies."

Donna began to cry. Though her hands were bound, Jamie shifted her body toward her sister, trying to comfort her. "Why are you doing this?" she asked.

"You haven't figured that out?" He leaned toward her. "Cops are so clueless. The Ice Cold Killer kills women, right? So killing a cop would be the ultimate. Your sister was just a way to get to you."

Jamie lay back on the bed, trying to memorize the details of her surroundings, searching for a way out. The room they were in wasn't very big, and seemed to be a combination kitchen, dining, living room and bedroom. A cabin, then. One of those Forest Service cabins where Alex and Tim had hidden before? Presumably when the second killer returned, they would kill Donna and Jamie, and transport them to the dump site. Or would they transport them first and kill them there? The latter provided more opportunities for escape, but she couldn't rely on that.

She would probably only have one chance to save her sister. She would have to be ready to take it, with no hesitation.

"WHERE'S JAMIE?" NATE ASKED, when he had finished searching the upstairs bedroom of the house, which had yielded no evidence that the two killers had ever been in there.

Dwight looked up from pulling books from the bookcase. "She went out to check the shed."

"You let her go out there alone?" Nate asked.

"I'd let you go out there alone," Dwight said.

Nate didn't bother answering but raced outside. The door of the shed stood open, and as he approached, he heard moaning.

Pi Calendri lay in a pool of blood on the floor of the garden shed, his head resting on the deck of a lawnmower, his feet on a sack of mulch. Nate pulled out a phone and called for an ambulance, then knelt beside the young man and tried to rouse him.

Pi's eyes flickered open. "It hurts bad," he said, his voice faint.

"Hang in there, buddy," Nate said. "Help is on the way." He examined the injury to the boy's shoulder. Pi had lost a lot of blood and he might be in shock, but the wound was a clean one. "Tell me what happened, so I can find out who did this."

"Those two climbers? I saw one this morning and figured they were in the neighborhood. I knew you were looking for them. I figured maybe they were the Ice Cold Killers. I figured I'd find them—you know, be a hero." He closed his eyes. "Guess I was really stupid."

"Stay with me," Nate said. "The ambulance will be here soon."

Pi moaned.

"Pi!" Nate patted his cheek and the young man opened his eyes. "Did you see a woman come in here? Just a little while ago."

"No, I haven't seen anything. Just help me, man, I'm scared."

"I'll help you, I promise," Nate said. "What did you see before you were shot?"

"I found the house. I knew it was the right one because I saw the Jeep in the garage. I looked through the back window and saw one of the guys with this chubby girl dressed all in pink. I was looking for a way into the garage. I thought maybe I'd disable the Jeep so they couldn't leave, you know? But when I got back here, the other one stepped out from the shed and just shot me."

"Did you overhear any conversation? Did they say where they were headed from here?"

Pi shook his head and closed his eyes again. "I didn't hear anything. It really hurts. Where's that ambulance?"

"It will be here soon."

The light changed and Nate turned to see Dwight in the doorway. "What happened to him?" he asked.

"Gunshot wound. The ambulance is on its way."

"Where's Jamie?"

"I don't know." Nate rose. "Stay with Pi, will you? I've got to go look for her."

He found Travis in the living room, on the phone. The sheriff ended the call. "I put out a BOLO on the Jeep, and there's already an Amber Alert for Donna."

"With the roads closed, we know they can't go far," Nate said.

"It's still a big county," Travis said.

"I think they'll go somewhere familiar," Nate said. "Some place they don't think we'll look, because we've looked there before."

"You think they'll go back to the summer cabins?" Travis asked.

"It makes the most sense," Nate said. "It's easy to get to, but away from other houses and people."

"Which cabins?" Travis asked.

"Sundance," Nate said. "They stayed there at least a few days, and the back way to the road makes it easier for them to get away. And they burned the Toyota there. They keep coming back to that location."

"Then let's go."

JAMIE FOCUSED ON keeping Tim talking. As long as she was talking, she and Donna were still alive. "What made you come to Eagle Mountain?" she asked. "You'd have a lot more targets in a big city like Denver."

"More cops, too," Tim said. "But coming here was my partner's idea. Some woman he knew was here and he wanted to see her. Then he realized how easy it would be to fool a little sheriff's department like this one. It was kind of an experiment, I guess."

"And you just went along with the idea of killing a bunch of women?" Jamie wasn't sure she did a good job of masking her disgust.

"Yeah, well, I was a little freaked out with the first one, but then, it was kind of a thrill, you know? Getting away with something, right under the cops' noses." He stood and walked over to the bed. "And now there'll be one less cop to follow us around."

Donna whimpered and pressed closer against Jamie, who could feel her shaking. "Is this really your sister?" Tim asked. "She doesn't look like you. Must be a drag, having to look after her."

"It's not a drag," Jamie said. "Donna is the most wonderful sister in the world. I'm very lucky to have her."

"Well, you won't have anything much longer. As soon as my friend gets back—" He made a slashing motion across his throat.

Donna began to sob again.

A phone rang and Tim answered. "Yeah? Where are you, man? I'm waiting…What? You're gonna make me deal with both of them?…No, I'm not saying I can't do it, just that that's not how this works. We're a team, aren't we?…All right, all right. I'll bring them and we can do them there. Where are you?" He glanced toward the window. "It's really coming down out there, isn't it?…Yeah, I know you like the snow 'cause it covers our tracks. It's still cold…All right. Be there in a few." He replaced the phone in his pocket. "Change of plans, ladies. We're gonna go for a little ride." He reached for Donna but as soon as he touched her, she screamed.

"Shut up!" He slapped her across the face, then pulled a bandanna from his pocket and stuffed it in her mouth. "You cooperate or I'll slit your throat right here." He shifted his gaze to Jamie. "And if you give me any trouble, I'll kill her first—slowly."

Jamie suppressed a shudder. For whatever reason, Alex had left Tim to deal with her and Donna on his own. That upped the odds in her favor. "Donna, honey, you do what he says," she said.

Tim hauled Donna to her feet. "That's better," he said. "Now I'm gonna put you in this chair by the door, then I'll get your sister. I'll tie the two of you together and cut loose your feet, then we'll all go out to the car. And remember, don't try anything." He pulled a small pistol from beneath his sweatshirt. "I can't miss from this close range."

Jamie's stomach clenched as she stared at the pistol, then she forced herself to look away. Even if he fired on her, he might not kill her. Some chance of staying alive was better than none. She braced herself and when he bent over to pull her to her feet, she resisted. "I'm caught on something," she said, pretending to try to raise up. "I think the tape on my wrists is hung up on a spring or something."

"What?" He bent over to take a closer look and she brought her knees up and hit him hard in the nose. A sickening crunch, and blood spurted across her. Tim screamed and dropped the pistol, clutching at his nose. He stumbled backward and Jamie struggled upright. She dived for the gun even as he reached for it, and then he was standing over her, kicking her and cursing. She dodged his blows and kicked out at the pistol, sending it skittering under the bed. Tim struck her hard on the side of the head. Her vision blurred and her stomach heaved. "Donna, run!" she shouted. "Hop or crawl if you have to, just leave."

Donna remained in her chair, tears streaming down her face. "Jamie, I can't leave you!"

"Donna, go!"

"Neither one of you are going anywhere." Tim had retrieved the gun and stood over her, the barrel of the pistol inches from her forehead. Jamie closed her eyes and thought of Nate—how she would never see him again, or get to tell him that she loved him. She'd been so foolish, wasting time being afraid of what might happen, instead of enjoying the time they had together.

The door to the cabin burst open and gunfire exploded. Jamie braced herself against the pain she was sure would come, but instead only felt hands reaching for her. She opened her eyes to find Nate beside her, slashing through the tape at her wrists and ankles. She threw her arms around him and he gathered her close. "Donna?" she asked.

"She's fine. Travis is helping her."

The tears she had been holding back for the last few hours burst forth. "I love you," she sobbed. "I'm sorry I didn't tell you before."

"Shhh." He patted her back, soothing her. "You didn't have to tell me," he said. "I knew."

"How did you know?" She stared at him through the tears.

"That day I saw you at the scavenger hunt on Travis's ranch, when you wouldn't even look at me. I knew I'd never stopped loving you—and that you wouldn't avoid me like that unless there were still some strong feelings buried somewhere."

"You were awfully sure of yourself," she said.

"I was sure you were the only woman for me," he said. "I had to go away to figure that out, but now I'm back to stay."

Jamie clutched his shoulder. "I come with a lot of baggage, you know."

He hugged her close. "Donna isn't baggage," he whispered. "She's an extra bonus. I never had a sister, you know."

"Am I gonna be your sister?" Donna knelt beside them.

"If you'll have me for a brother," Nate said.

"I think you'd better ask Jamie if she'll have you for a husband," Donna said. "That's the way it's supposed to work, you know. You propose to your girlfriend, not her sister."

Jamie almost laughed out loud at the expression on Nate's face, but he recovered quickly and took her hand. "What about it, Jamie?" he asked. "Will you marry me?"

"Yes." She kissed him.

"Yes!" Donna said and kissed him, too.

Someone cleared his throat, and Jamie looked up to see the sheriff standing over them. "Tim Dawson is dead," he said. "Do you know where Alex Woodruff is?"

"He called and told Tim to meet him somewhere, and to bring us with him," Jamie said. "But I don't know where." She looked at Nate. "Did you shoot Tim?"

"If I hadn't, he would have killed you," he said.

She nodded. "Yes."

"Maybe we can trace Alex through Tim's phone," Travis said. "We'll gather what evidence we can here. In the meantime, Nate, will you take Jamie and her sister home?"

"I should stay and help," Jamie said, trying to scramble to her feet.

"Take care of your sister first," Travis said. "That's an order, Deputy."

"Yes, sir." She would take care of Donna. She and Nate together. They would be a family. Amazing how wonderful that sounded.

Ice Cold Killer Claims Another Victim

A twenty-three-year-old local woman is the Ice Cold Killer's latest victim, after her body was found in her vehicle on County Road Seven early Tuesday morning. Her identity has not been released, pending notification of her next of kin.

Sheriff Travis Walker announced Monday evening that Timothy Dawson, 21, who was one of the chief suspects in the string of murders that have shocked Rayford County over the past few weeks, was killed during a confrontation with law enforcement officers. Dawson's accomplice remains at large and, as the latest murder seems to indicate, intends to continue his killing spree.

* * * * *

Look for the conclusion of Cindi Myers's
Eagle Mountain Murder Mystery:
Deadly Wedding miniseries,
Snowblind Justice,
available next month.

And don't miss the previous titles in the series:
Ice Cold Killer
Snowbound Suspicion

Available now from Harlequin Intrigue!

COMING NEXT MONTH FROM

H HARLEQUIN®

INTRIGUE

Available October 22, 2019

#1887 ENEMY INFILTRATION
Red, White and Built: Delta Force Deliverance • by Carol Ericson
Horse trainer Lana Moreno refuses to believe her brother died during an
attack on the embassy outpost he was guarding. Her last hope to uncover
the truth is Delta Force soldier Logan Hess, who has his own suspicions
about the attack. Can they survive long enough to discover what happened?

#1888 RANSOM AT CHRISTMAS
Rushing Creek Crime Spree • by Barb Han
Kelly Morgan has been drugged, and the only thing she can remember
is that she's in danger. When rancher Will Kent finds her on his ranch, he
immediately takes her to safety, putting himself in the sights of a murderer
in the process.

#1889 SNOWBLIND JUSTICE
Eagle Mountain Murder Mystery: Winter Storm Wedding
by Cindi Myers
Brodie Langtry, an investigator with the Colorado Bureau of Investigation, is
in town to help with the hunt for the Ice Cold Killer. He's shocked when he
discovers that Emily Walker, whom he hasn't seen in years, is the murderer's
next target.

#1890 WARNING SHOT
Protectors at Heart • by Jenna Kernan
Sheriff Axel Trace is not sure Homeland Security agent Rylee Hockings's
presence will help him keep the peace in his county. But when evidence
indicates that a local terrorist group plans to transport a virus over the
US-Canadian border, the two must set aside their differences to save their
country.

#1891 RULES IN DECEIT
Blackhawk Security • by Nichole Severn
Network analyst Elizabeth Dawson thought she'd moved on from the
betrayal that destroyed her career—that is, until Braxton Levitt shows up one
day claiming there's a target on her back only he can protect her against.

#1892 WITNESS IN THE WOODS
by Michele Hauf
Conservation officer Joe Cash protects all kinds of endangered creatures,
but the stakes have never been higher. Now small-animal vet Skylar Davis
is seeking Joe's protection after being targeted by the very poachers he's
investigating.

**YOU CAN FIND MORE INFORMATION ON UPCOMING HARLEQUIN® TITLES,
FREE EXCERPTS AND MORE AT WWW.HARLEQUIN.COM.**

HICNM1019

"Let's try this again." Logan wiped his dusty palm against his shirt and held out his hand. "I'm Captain Logan Hess with US Delta Force."

Her mouth formed an O but at least she took his hand this time in a firm grip, her skin rough against his. "I'm Lana Moreno, but you probably already know that, don't you?"

"I sure do." He jerked his thumb over his shoulder. "I saw your little impromptu news conference about an hour ago."

"But you knew who I was before that. You didn't track me down to compare cowboy boots." She jabbed him in the chest with her finger. "Did you know Gilbert?"

"Unfortunately, no." Lana didn't need to know just how unfortunate that really was. "Let's get out of the dirt and grab some lunch."

She tilted her head and a swathe of dark hair fell over her shoulder, covering one eye. The other eye scorched his face. "Why should I have lunch with you? What do you want from me? When I heard you were Delta Force, I thought you might have known Gilbert, might've known what happened at that outpost."

"I didn't, but I know of Gilbert and the rest of them, even the assistant ambassador who was at the outpost. I can guarantee I know a lot more about the entire situation than you do from reading that redacted report they grudgingly shared with you."

"You are up-to-date. What are we waiting for?" Her feet scrambled beneath her as she slid up the wall. "If you have any information about the attack in Nigeria, I want to hear it."

"I thought you might." He rose from the ground, towering over her petite frame. He pulled a handkerchief from the inside pocket of his leather jacket and waved it at her. "Take this."

"Thank you." She blew her nose and mopped her face, running a corner of the cloth beneath each eye to clean up her makeup. "I suppose you don't want it back."

"You can wash it for me and return it the next time we meet."

That statement earned him a hard glance from those dark eyes, still sparkling with unshed tears, but he had every intention of seeing Lana Moreno again and again—however many times it took to pick her brain about why she believed there was more to the story than a bunch of Nigerian criminals deciding to attack an embassy outpost. It was a ridiculous cover story if he ever heard one.

About as ridiculous as the story of Major Rex Denver working with terrorists.

Her quest had to be motivated by more than grief over a brother. People didn't stage stunts like she just did in front of a congressman's office based on nothing.

Don't miss
Enemy Infiltration *by Carol Ericson,*
available November 2019 wherever
Harlequin® Intrigue *books and ebooks are sold.*

www.Harlequin.com

Need an adrenaline rush from nail-biting tales
(and irresistible males)?

Check out **Harlequin Intrigue®**,
Harlequin® Romantic Suspense and
Love Inspired® Suspense books!

New books available every month!

CONNECT WITH US AT:

Facebook.com/groups/HarlequinConnection

 Facebook.com/HarlequinBooks

Twitter.com/HarlequinBooks

 Instagram.com/HarlequinBooks

Pinterest.com/HarlequinBooks

ReaderService.com

**ROMANCE WHEN
YOU NEED IT**

SGENRE2018R